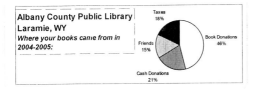

MY FACE
TO THE WIND

THE DIARY OF SARAH JANE
PRICE, A PRAIRIE TEACHER

BY JIM MURPHY

Scholastic Inc. New York

BROKEN BOW, NEBRASKA
1881

WEDNESDAY, DECEMBER 22, 1881

Dear Little Book,

Father said if I write in this diary I will see the world differently. But with Father gone my world is nothing but wind and dry grass, more wind and more dry grass. And an empty feeling inside.

Oh, Miss Kizer is nice, but she's always worrying. I can see it in her eyes even if she doesn't say it. Doesn't think Broken Bow a fit place for a 14-year-old girl alone. Last night she said she wished I had family to go to. She looked very concerned. "Are you sure you don't have blood relatives back East you could live with? A cousin of a cousin or such?"

Said I was sure. "Father said they were all dead."

When I said that, I thought about Father being dead from the black diptheria fever now two months and nine days, and that my mother was dead, and all my grandparents and other relatives too. Then I knew how alone I really was and I got angry again at Father for bringing me here and for getting sick, felt bad about being angry at him, and started to cry. Which I hate to do.

"Everything will be fine, dear," Miss Kizer said quickly. Though her eyes didn't seem to agree. She took our plates and hurried into the kitchen. "I'll find a good home for you," she added as she started to clean the dishes. "Don't you worry, dear, okay?"

"Okay," I sniffed.

Miss Kizer's cat — Grace — jumped up on the empty seat and glared at me with suspicious green eyes. As if I'd taken some of her precious food.

I waved my napkin in Grace's face, but she didn't move. Didn't even blink. Just sat there with her tiny eyes on me. Finally, I tossed my napkin right in her face. Then I went to my room to listen to the dry shivering of the long grass being pushed this way and that by the wind. And to write this.

I'm not sure how writing in this diary will change anything, but I will write in it again. Because I promised Father. I do know that if the Broken Bow school board hadn't made Father their teacher, he wouldn't have gotten sick. Wouldn't have died. If we hadn't come here, everything would be different now.

THURSDAY, DECEMBER 23, 1881

Dear Little Book,

Miss Kizer had me doing chores. Said, "Idle hands are the Devil's playground," as she sent me out to get water at the town well. I'm a paying boarder at Miss Kizer's, but I don't mind helping her. She looks older than her 42 years and always seems tired. Even when she's sitting in the parlor reading her Bible. Besides, she was kind to me while Father was sick with the fever. And after. Helping out is the least I can do.

The path to the well wanders around a number of sod houses, some solidly built with real windows, others little more than heaps of piled-up grass. Didn't see a single person out. Only some hens pecking the dry dirt and the Womeldorfs' skinny old dog scratching at his ear.

When we first got here last August there was lots of building going on, lots of activity. But since the fever visited, everything has stopped and everyone is inside — either sick or taking care of the sick. People still go out sometimes. To the well or Mr. Pelham's store or Mr. Tilling's bank, for instance. But they move quickly and don't spend much time chatting.

Got to the well and pumped the handle to draw up the water. Father said he took the teaching job here because Broken Bow had "prospects" and would grow big. Especially after the CB&Q Railroad comes through.

Filled the bucket, then looked around again. Still no one in sight. Even the animals had disappeared. Broken Bow certainly seems to be out of prospects these days.

The well isn't far from Miss Kizer's. Maybe 800 feet. I wasn't halfway home when the moaning of the wind made the town seem so still it was as if I was the only person left. Which is when the oddest thought came to me. I suddenly felt like screaming as loud as I could. To drive away the eerie emptiness. To let Broken Bow know that I hate it.

Just then, a door slammed somewhere off behind me and I remembered there were town folk inside all of the soddys. And they would hear me. That thought stopped me from calling out and I scurried home. Though it won't be home much longer if Miss Kizer has her way! That is all there is to write today.

SATURDAY, DECEMBER 24, 1881

Dear Little Book,

More chores today, so my hands were never a temptation for the Devil. When I finished, I read four poems from one of Father's favorite books. By Mr. Ralph Waldo Emerson.

Father knew lots of poems by lots of writers and loved to recite them — and he was the one who said this — "when the call is upon me." Mostly this happened when he was teaching a class, but not always.

Once back in Pennsylvania, we were crossing a little bridge near where we were staying. We'd gone about halfway across when Father suddenly stopped and began saying one of Mr. Emerson's poems about the Revolution.

I was always embarrassed when he did this. And he did it a lot.

I repeated the opening lines in a whisper hoping to bring Father back into my head fully. "By the rude bridge that arched the flood / Their flag to April's breeze unfurled / Here once the embattled farmers stood / And fired the shot heard round the world. . . ."

It didn't work. Father had a way of making every word, every line, seem bigger and more important than I could ever hope to do. As if they'd come from the Holy Book itself.

After this, I went to the back door where the thermometer said it was 53 degrees. If it goes like this much longer, there will be no winter at all this year. Just then, Mr. Bock went past on long, wobbly legs. Mr. Bock works a still down by the river, and it looked as if he'd been testing his product.

He spotted me and fumbled to tip his hat. "Good day to you, Miss," he called out loudly. Though it was half in German, half in mixed-up English, so it came out "Guden day too yoo, Missee." But his voice sounded cheerful, something I hadn't heard in weeks. He must have finally recognized who I was because his smile faded and his face turned serious. "We miss him, you know. The town misses its teacher. Must be hard, it being Christmas." He put on his hat and went on his way, mumbling, "A shame. Such a shame."

That's the way it's been lately. I might be reading something and enjoying it and then I think about Father and feel sad all over again. Not even Christmas can change that.

MONDAY, DECEMBER 26, 1881

Dear Little Book,

The strangest thing. My eyes popped open in the middle of the night. I was wide-awake in a second, surrounded by blackness. Not a sliver of light anywhere. And then I heard Father.

Least, I think it was his voice, it was so faint and distant. Not talking either. Singing. In his high, reedy voice that always went cracking. Singing that hymn he loved from *The Praise Book*: "Soon we'll reach the shining river / Soon our pilgrimage shall cease / Soon our happy hearts will quiver / With the melody of Peace."

The last time he'd sung that was when the stagecoach we were on was a few miles outside of Broken Bow. Father is . . . was very tall and his legs were crammed into that little compartment along with me and the other passengers and some packages and boxes. So when he sang the hymn he substituted the word "leg" for "hearts." But why was he singing it now?

Then the singing stopped and the next instant there was Father. I really saw him! Teaching a class last year in Harlan, Iowa.

It was late May, I recall, and so warm that he had the door wide open to let in a cool breeze. I was in the back of the room helping a 7-year-old girl with her numbers when I noticed that the bright light coming in the door was flooding over Father, turning him a translucent white so intense it was blinding.

So far what I was seeing was exactly as it took place. Then something happened that was new. Father glanced in my direction and pointed to the book I was holding. I looked at the book, then back to him, and he smiled and gave me an approving wink.

Why are you pointing to the book? I wanted to ask. But at that moment a gust of wind slammed the door shut with a ferocious bang and he vanished, and it was as if all the air had gone out of me. That I'd been drained of everything alive. And then I woke up all over again. Only this time it was daytime.

Strange. It was so real and scary too. But I want him to visit again.

LATER IN THE MORNING

Told Miss Kizer about hearing Father sing and seeing him. She didn't say anything at first, but her eyes darted around the room nervously. As if a hungry wolf had gotten in and she was looking for a place to hide. Then she changed the subject and started talking about Reverend Lauter's visit and how she was looking forward to it.

But I wanted to know what she thought — about *Father's* visit — and I asked her straight out.

She looked troubled, then she let loose one of her deeper sighs. "It was just a dream, Sarah Jane. And the wind. That's all."

I was going to tell her I was sure it was more than just a dream. The singing had been distant, hard to hear, but I had seen Father, no question about it. And what he did — his pointing to the book, his smile and the wink — was completely different from what had really happened.

"Was he trying to tell me something?" I asked.

Either she didn't hear or didn't want to because Miss Kizer went on to say that the wind sings a lot. Just about every day. And it talks, and it huffs and puffs, and it sometimes screams and laughs. She said it can change the way a person thinks and dreams. "Sarah Jane," she said. "Best pay no mind to that wind or you'll wind up like Johnnie Hatter."

Johnnie Hatter one day started talking to himself morning to night, arguing and shaking his fist in the air and carrying on in a way that scared everybody in town, including the horses and dogs. Then on his 30th birthday he set fire to his sod house and went to live in a cave in the riverbank. Just up from Mr. Bock's still. That was in August and Johnnie's still there and still talking to himself.

Miss Kizer thought it could have been Johnnie out singing

to the stars the way he does some nights. That maybe the wind pushed a gate shut and I used that in my dream. She asked, "It's possible, isn't it?" Saying everybody hears things in the wind out here and everybody learns to ignore it. I should too.

Everybody? I thought. Which made me wonder what sort of things Miss Kizer heard and saw. Of course I didn't ask her. She still had that scared, nervous look on her face and I didn't want to stir up bad memories for her.

Gave her a half smile as a response instead. But I will tell you, Little Book, something that came into my head then. I'm not sure I want to ignore my dream. I need to talk with Father and see him smile again.

Friday, December 30, 1881

Dear Little Book,

No dreams or singing these last few nights. Every morning I sit at breakfast wondering why Father hasn't reappeared and every morning Miss Kizer asks why I look so thoughtful. Can't tell her what is on my mind, so I shake my head and make believe I'm interested in what is on my plate.

The moment I finished breakfast today Miss Kizer put me to work and hard — bringing in water, sweeping out the rooms, putting clean linen on beds. And collecting cow chips to burn in the stoves. Miss Kizer calls the chips Nebraska coal — as if a change in name makes it something other than dried plop!

"Everything needs to be spotless," she explained and she was very excited. "Reverend Lauter will be here any day. Emmett Tilling saw him up to Anselmo 3 weeks past which means we're next on his route after Merna."

At least she didn't begin the day by worrying over where else I could live.

Then she started telling me how Reverend Lauter travels up the Middle Loup River as far as Dunning, heads south to Anselmo, then down Muddy Creek Valley to Broken Bow and other towns until he gets to Rockville. After this stop he heads back up the Middle Loup to do his circuit all over again, though sometimes he travels along as far as Grand Island.

I knew all this and said so. When the black diphtheria hit Broken Bow and Father died, Reverend Lauter was miles away. I remember feeling angry that he hadn't hurried to be with me when I needed him, until Miss Kizer explained where his traveling took him. I realized then it was foolish to expect him to come running back just for me. Once you leave town, the land opens up so big it's as if you've gone to another planet.

Miss Kizer went on about his travels anyway. I suppose to keep my mind off Father and hers off . . . off what?

Saturday, December 31, 1881

Dear Little Book,

Took the wheelbarrow to gather more Nebraska coal. It was as warm today as the rest of winter — 48 degrees — and for once there was hardly any wind, so I didn't need a coat, only a wool sweater. Did wear gloves since picking up chips is not my idea of fun.

Stopped by the cemetery to visit Father and to think about things. Was that you the other night, Father? Or was it like Miss Kizer said? A little bit Johnnie Hatter, a little bit ordinary dream, all made funny by the wind.

Only I've had dreams before and this one was different. You were so clear and distinct this time. So how do I puzzle out the truth?

But standing there, my head didn't do much worthwhile puzzling. At least none that helped answer my questions. I just stared at Father's grave — with grass beginning to poke through the dirt like whiskers on a chin, the wood-cross marker raw and very fresh. The same as the fourteen other new crosses in the tiny cemetery. Thanks to the fever.

Said good-bye to Father, then wandered down the path that leads through town. Or what there is of town. Only 30 buildings have been put up so far, scattered around without any order.

Miss Kizer's boardinghouse is the biggest structure in

Broken Bow. Made of unpainted wood and 2 stories tall with 6 rooms. Most houses are tiny soddys. The few businesses in town — the bank, blacksmith, land office, the feed store and livery, lawyer's office, and saloon — are nothing but canvas tents with wood fronts.

People want to see if the town will survive before paying to bring in lumber. When I learned that, I asked Miss Kizer why she'd built with milled wood. All she said was that she needed more than prairie grass between her and the outside world.

Scared. That's what Miss Kizer is, plain and simple. Of the fever and the wind and whatever else she hears and dreams.

Must have been thinking hard on this because the next moment I looked up and let out a surprised yelp. Somebody was standing right in front of my wheelbarrow.

"I'm sorry. Really I am," the person said real quick as she came around to my side. "I didn't mean to scare you, honest. My father says I always walk Indian-like. But I don't do it on purpose."

It was Ida Pelham, who is 10 years old, but as tall as me. And a chatterbox besides. Unlike most people I've met here who say hello and good-bye and not much in between.

"Why did you do that!" I screamed, even though I'd heard her apologize.

I said some other things — loudly — and Ida apologized

and asked if I was all right over and over again until I was embarrassed for having carried on so.

Felt worse when I remembered Father once said that people who talked and talked were usually nervous and that sometimes their words flew ahead of their thinking.

I thought the same when I first met Ida a few days after we'd gotten to Broken Bow. She was friendly, but she really did fill up the air with words. So many that I couldn't follow her at times. And she was young besides. I'd hoped to meet girls more my age, so I didn't go looking for Ida after that first meeting. Then the fever was here and, well, not much visiting has gone on since.

"I saw you come from the cemetery," she said. "It must be sad. About your father." She went on saying she wouldn't know what she'd do if her mother or father had died. Or even Timothy, her pesky brother. Though most days she wished he'd take a long trip.

I suddenly felt uncomfortable. Wasn't sure I wanted to talk about these things with somebody I hardly knew. Then I thought about how Miss Kizer always grows uneasy if I mention Father. Ida, at least, didn't seem afraid of the conversation.

So I told her I went to talk with him.

Her eyes were big and round with surprise, so I said, "Not really talk. More like I go and think about things . . . about him . . ." I stopped here because this was where Miss Kizer would begin talking about something else. Ida was just looking at me, waiting. So I told her I try to remember him from before we came to Broken Bow and before he got sick. "Sometimes" — and here I cautioned myself, remembering how Miss Kizer had acted — "a few nights ago . . . I think I saw and heard him." I glanced quick at Ida, but her expression hadn't changed much. She was listening carefully, that's all. So I told her it was probably just a dream, but it seemed real then.

"Like a ghost," Ida said in a hushed voice. "Or an angel." She said that her parents don't believe much in angels, but she does. She thinks they watch over us and try to tell us things and make us do good deeds. Only the bad angels are trying to make us do bad things at the same time. But she's sure my father is a good angel.

"Yes," I said softly.

"And your mother too. My mother gives me the devil sometimes, but then she looks sorry and apologizes and makes everything better. What was she like?" When I looked confused, Ida added, "Your mother. What was she like?" She knew she passed a long time back because Ida had heard her parents talking.

Told her I didn't know much. Father didn't like talking about Mother, it made him so sad. I always thought there would be time when I got older to ask, so I never pressed him to describe her. Told Ida she died when I was 4, so I didn't remember her, except that Father had said she was pretty and had long brown hair. Like mine. And that she was the smartest person he had ever met. He said that a lot. She was very practical, he told me once.

There were a few more details about my mother that I knew from Father. That she played the piano, always remembered people's names, and that she had lots of friends. But I didn't tell Ida any of this. Because I suddenly realized how very little I knew about her, how very little Father had told me. Why, I wondered, had he kept all the other things about Mother to himself?

I must have looked upset because Ida suddenly took the wheelbarrow handles from me, began pushing it up the path, and telling me she knew a good spot for chips, out of town a ways.

I was glad she'd gotten us moving again. It wasn't that I minded talking about my parents as angels. I just didn't like the idea that they were floating all around and I couldn't talk to them when I wanted to.

We came to the place where Ida collected chips, on a creek a mile or so north of Broken Bow. There are little scrubby trees in and around town, but out here there are none and the land opens out like a rolling ocean. The first time I stood and really looked at the grass I got so dizzy I had to sit down.

Ida explained that ranchers let their herds drink at this spot before driving them across. That was why it was usually a good spot for chips. I started to reach for a really big one when

Ida shouted, "Watch out for fresh pies!" Then she showed me how to check them with a stick before picking them up. "Sometimes, the outside is hard, but the inside is still —" her stick broke through the hard crust to a soft center and her nose crinkled in disgust "— gummy."

After the wheelbarrow was loaded up heavy we headed back to town, Ida talking away the whole time. Funny thing is that I didn't mind her chatter as much.

LATER

I will be as brief as possible as I am tired. Spent the rest of the day getting Reverend Lauter's room ready. Read a little too. From that book of poems.

At dinner Miss Kizer talked about how last year the house was bursting on New Year's eve. A man from the railroad, a cattleman, somebody from the state land claims office, and a homesteading husband and wife. I could tell she was remembering those busy, cheerful days. When she didn't have to worry about a 14-year-old girl.

"People will come back," I said. "Soon as the fever's all gone and the railroad starts laying track. You'll see."

She said the railroad was supposed to be through here 8 months ago, and now they aren't scheduled to reach Broken Bow for 5 or 6 months. And that supposes they don't run out of money again. She shook her head thoughtfully. "I don't mind telling you that money is growing tight. If it runs out, how am I to pay for supplies and such?"

I opened my mouth to say she could probably get credit at Mr. Pelham's store like the Bocks do, but thought better of it. Miss Kizer once said that borrowing more than a cup of sugar was the first step down the path of ruin and that Mr. Bock was proof sure of this.

Miss Kizer made tea and when she sat down again Grace jumped onto her lap and settled in for a nap.

"The Lord will provide," she said, nodding her head. "The Bible says that and I believe it. Just as I know we'll find a place for you somewhere, and we'll find it soon. All we have to do is pray."

That may have comforted Miss Kizer, but praying didn't work for me with Father. Besides, her words sounded as if I was going to be shipped off like an unwanted package.

Said good night a little after this and went to my room. Every time I come in here I'm struck by how little I have left of Father. His clothes were burned after he died, as was his traveling bag, shaving kit, and wallet. Am left with his gold watch, which sits on my night table unwound and still, and all 22 of his books. Tried to read one of his history books, but didn't get very far in it.

Father kept his books in near-perfect condition. Oh, you could tell they had been read over and over again because their spines didn't crack when you opened them. But the pages are spotless. I was reading along just fine until I turned a page and saw the smudge at the bottom.

It wasn't heavy or dark and it didn't blot out any words. Still, I had to close the book and take a deep breath. Last New Year's eve I had Father with me. Now all I have of him is a faint print of his finger.

TUESDAY, JANUARY 3, 1882

Dear Little Book,

Heard sawing and hammering from over near Mr. Tilling's bank, the first real building noise in a long while. So I went to see what was happening.

2 men I didn't know had brought in a wagon of cut boards and were beginning to put up a building frame. When I asked what kind of store it would be, the younger man spit out a stream of brown tobacco juice and laughed. "Why, heck, Miss," he told me while his jaw worked away. "This is jest a shed fer tools and such. A buncha fellas from Grand Island is putting up this hotel fer cattlemen. 20 rooms."

"I heard 30," his partner corrected him. "It'll be made of brick too. You can believe it or not, I don't care."

I left the men arguing and hurried back to tell Miss Kizer the news, all the while thinking, she's not going to like it one little bit.

But I could tell the moment I walked in that she already

knew about the hotel. News — especially the bad kind — seems to travel along fast around here.

"I run a good, honest establishment, so I'm not worried," she said, looking very worried. Grace wandered in and stared at me as if I was the one building the hotel. Miss Kizer said people knew she had clean sheets and gave good value for the price. Said she'd do just fine, no matter.

But her eyes looked confused and frightened, and she didn't even pick up Grace when she rubbed against her legs. Instead, she took out her Bible and hugged it.

I wasn't sure what to do, so I stood there too. And so did Grace. It was as if everything had frozen in place. Then Miss Kizer had me strip all the beds of their linens so she could wash them again. She could build her house to keep out the wind, but I guess it couldn't keep out the competition.

SATURDAY, JANUARY 7, 1882

Dear Little Book,

This morning Miss Kizer announced that she'd finally figured out what to do with me. At breakfast she sighed several times and said, "I've thought a lot about our problem, Sarah Jane, and prayed for proper guidance."

Of course, it wasn't *our* problem. It was *mine* — where I would live.

She had her Bible on the table and pulled an envelope from it. "I've written this letter to the Orphan Girls Asylum over to Grand Island. To see if they have a place there for you." She put on a smile, but it seemed thin and forced to me. Said she didn't know much about it but some in town praised it highly, so she was sure it's a fine institution. They would give me a good education, something I couldn't get around here.

Miss Kizer went on describing the wonders of Grand Island but I didn't hear much. The words "Orphan Girls Asylum" kept repeating and banging around in my head. And every time I heard them, they sounded more awful. Orphan Girls Asylum. Orphan Girls. Orphan. Asylum.

I actually started to shake a little and feel afraid. As if a stagecoach would pull up to the door any second and I'd be pushed aboard and gone in minutes.

"But . . ." I stammered, "I can still pay. I still have money in Mr. Tilling's bank."

Miss Kizer said she knew, but that money will run out eventually, won't it? And just now she's in no position . . . with business so slow and that new hotel. . . . She had a tired look to her brown eyes. In a quiet voice she added that the Orphan Girls Asylum was the best way that she could think of. The only way really. She held the letter up. Said we need to contact them now, before any snow falls.

Before my money runs out is more like it, I thought, as an angry feeling swept over me.

When Father died he had 56 dollars and 28 cents left in Mr. Tilling's bank. This wasn't a lot of money but it was enough to keep us at Miss Kizer's until the spring school term started. Then Father would get a portion of his pay in advance — enough to rent a sod house and buy food and such for a while.

That was his plan anyway. Father always had a plan.

After he died, Miss Kizer lowered the room and board from $2.90 to $2.10 a week. Which Miss Kizer said is fair, but I thought a little high since I don't really eat very much. Then Mr. Gaddis — who is the head of the school board — said he was sorry but Father owed the town the 20 dollars advanced to him for our railroad fare. So now I only have enough left in the bank to stay here 8 weeks and a dribble more.

If I had more money, Miss Kizer wouldn't be so worried. Or in such a hurry to pack me off to that Orphan Girls Asylum on Grand Island.

That last bit suddenly registered. Like a sharp jab in the side. I'd assumed that I'd wind up someplace in town or in a home within walking distance of Broken Bow. But Grand Island is 80 or 90 miles from here. From Father. I'd have to leave him in that tiny cemetery with nobody to visit him.

LATER

As soon as Miss Kizer went to give the letter to Mr. Hewitt, I decided to go for a walk. To figure out how I could stay in Broken Bow.

Father always said a good walk will clear the mind and open it up to sensible answers.

Went along the creek, past Wilson Hewitt's dugout with the painted sign over the door saying Broken Bow Post Office. Said hello to Mrs. Bock. She takes in clothes from the bachelors in and near town and there was a basket piled high with laundry. While she hung a shirt out to dry, her 2 boys, Jason and Huey, were racing around screaming and the baby was pulling up fistfuls of grass.

Mrs. Bock stopped what she was doing, squinted hard at me, gave me a tiny nod, said, "Mornin', Sarah Jane," and went back to her chore. I wonder if she ever smiles?

Walked out of town as far as the old buffalo trail and stood looking at the deep ruts made by thousands of animals over thousands of years, though I've never seen one of the creatures myself.

To stay I needed to earn money. But instead of thinking about that I suddenly remembered back to early September and the time Father and I visited the buffalo trail together.

He said he wanted to show me something special, and he

brought me to these wide, deep gullies. They were startling to see stretching as they did from one horizon to the other and packed so hard only a little stubbly grass grew in them.

Then he started to talk about history. About the trail being real history and not just the book kind. How the buffalo lived off the grassland for thousands of years. Then the Indians came and lived off the buffalo. "Some people call them savages." I remember Father telling me. "But they're a strong race of people."

Father loved to talk about the Indians and often went on at great length to describe their customs and traditions — how they set up communities in this emptiness, formed tribal governments, established rituals and passed them along through hundreds of generations, and how white men had driven them off their homelands.

You would hardly know they lived here, he explained. They kept their history in their heads and shared it in spoken stories. "So many of the Indians have been lost to the white man's diseases and the white man's guns," he said, "and sadly, so has a great deal of their history."

That was when he gave you to me, Little Book, and made me promise to write in you every day.

Only I didn't. Didn't think anything in Broken Bow was worth writing down.

Lost all thought of the past when the Hewitt boys, Fred and Edwin, came over a nearby hill at that moment. I said hi and both boys grunted "hey" as a greeting. The 2 continued their journey a few steps when Fred turned and called, "You'll be waiting there a long time before any buffalo go by."

Fred and Edwin must have thought this the funniest thing ever said because they started laughing and I could still hear them guffawing as they disappeared from sight.

Now I wish I had written in you from the start. So I could have captured Father like he was when we visited the buffalo trail that day. Or hear him saying a poem out loud to embarrass me. Instead, I've got the Hewitt boys down on paper. So that 100 years from now some reader I don't know can see how dumb they were!

LATER STILL

So much for thought-making walks! Father seemed to come up with answers to problems whenever he had to, but by dinnertime all I could think to say was, "Maybe I could help out around here. To pay for my room. Do chores. Help with . . . things."

Miss Kizer clucked in disapproval, and said that it wasn't that easy. When the cold set in — and it would — the price of everything would go up. She had money to last a while, but not much more. And without boarders . . .

Miss Kizer was interrupted by the ringing of the mantel clock, which was just as well because I got the point. She wasn't going to be talked out of her Orphan Girls Asylum plan. Not unless I could earn enough real money to stay and not worry her.

Father would figure out a solution and make it work. Like the time we were traveling through Iowa on the railroad and our money ran so low that it looked as if we would go without food. At least until we reached Harlan where Father's next teaching job — and the advance on his salary — waited.

I was scared and hungry. But Father said not to worry and that everything would be fine. At the next town — I think it was called Marengo — we were strolling down a crowded street and all of a sudden Father took off his hat, held it over his heart, and started reciting poems. Out in the open for strangers to see and hear! And then he passed his hat around and collected enough coins for several meals.

I can recite poems too. Plenty of them. Father was always drilling me to remember poems. But I doubt there's much call for them here in Broken Bow. So what else can I do to earn some money? Maybe Father will appear again to help me figure out an answer. Or maybe I need to take another long walk — this time away from the buffalo trails!

THURSDAY, JANUARY 12, 1882

Dear Little Book,

Reverend Lauter arrived after dark today and is to have a

prayer meeting at Rose and James Gandy's home on Sunday. He is an odd sort of man, the Reverend is. Short with big ears, snow-white hair that looks like angry ocean waves, and the darkest pair of eyes I have ever seen. Bet he sees sin everywhere with them!

When he first came in the door, he put his dusty canvas bag down, took both of Miss Kizer's hands in his, and looked into her eyes. He pronounced every word slowly and carefully in a hushed voice. "Sister Kizer, I am so thankful this plague has passed you over. So very thankful."

Can't say that I took to his overly dramatic ways. It might have been what Father once said after listening to a man named Walter Chalmers going on about the health benefits of a bottle of his Chalmers Old Time Bitters. "For all those fancy words of his," Father said as we walked away, "he never once guaranteed that his concoction would work, and he never said he would give back your money if it didn't. Straight talk, Sarah Jane, usually comes from an honest tongue."

So I wasn't prepared for what happened when Miss Kizer introduced me to the Reverend and told him about Father. Reverend Lauter took a sweeping step toward me and I immediately decided I wasn't going to give him my hands to hold like Miss Kizer had. Instead he rested the fingers of his right hand on my left shoulder and looked right at me with those sin-seeking eyes of his. "Brother Tilling mentioned that the new teacher had passed." His eyes seemed suddenly to fill with sadness, like Father's whenever he mentioned my mother. "What a terrible loss for you, Sarah Jane. What a terrible loss for all of the children of Broken Bow."

I noticed then that a gentle warmth was radiating from the spot where his fingers were touching my shoulder and my mouth went dry. I didn't know what to say so I looked down.

"These things don't happen without reason," he added. "It's hard to believe this at first. God's way is often a mystery to us. Especially when that way is so tragic and painful."

I didn't understand how any good could come from Father being dead and the Reverend's words certainly weren't going to bring Father back to me. But they did feel comforting. In a way.

I showed the Reverend his room, which is upstairs directly over mine, while Miss Kizer boiled up water for tea. Then we all sat around the table in the front parlor room drinking our tea and talking, with Grace nuzzled peacefully in Miss Kizer's lap.

Or rather, Miss Kizer and Reverend Lauter talked — Miss Kizer about the fever and how it'd run through town and the outlying farms, the Reverend about his travels and what he'd seen along the way. Seems that at least 2 other towns, Merna and Dunning, have the black diphtheria and that another small town asked the Reverend to skip over them this time for fear he might infect their people.

I am writing this in my room and fighting to keep my eyes

open long enough to finish. The Reverend is in his room above me, walking back and forth very slowly. As if he's lost and trying to find his way. Or maybe walking helps him think too. Like Father. Still do not know what I feel about him, and am too tired now to work it through. I have more important things to figure out anyway. And so good night.

MIDDLE OF THE NIGHT

Thought I heard him again. Father. Not singing this time. Talking. Couldn't make out the words at all, but I'm sure it was him and I'm sure he was trying to say something to me. But what? I have so many questions to ask him now, so many things I need to know. I am going to stay up and listen very carefully. Which is why I've lit my lamp and am writing. To copy down what he says exactly.

FRIDAY, JANUARY 13, 1882

Dear Little Book,

I stayed awake a long time — I heard the mantel clock chime 2:00, 2:15, 2:30. The wind did make noise, as always — a low moaning, like a big sleeping bear breathing in her cave. The grass chattered away too. But nothing from Father.

Drifted off to sleep and then bolted awake when I heard a

voice. But it was only Johnnie Hatter drifting past my window, talking to himself and making a strange sort of snuffling sound.

LATER IN THE MORNING

I am in my room, cloak and bonnet on and ready to leave for the Bocks', but I had to write this first to get it out of my head. Otherwise I will be spitting mad all day.

When I went in for breakfast, Reverend Lauter was at the table with Miss Kizer talking in a low voice. They stopped when they saw me and Miss Kizer had a funny expression on her face. The kind you get when you've been caught doing something naughty.

The Reverend stood, held a chair for me and said good morning, drawing out the words in a deep, rich voice. He also flashed a welcoming smile.

Miss Kizer looked nervous and then blurted out that she and the Reverend had been talking about my situation, and that he knew someone at the Asylum.

The Reverend nodded vigorously and said that he and the headmaster, a Mr. Talbot Williams, were friends and that he often visited the Asylum to pray with the staff and the girls. "It's a fine Christian institution."

Miss Kizer added quickly that the Reverend had agreed to write a special note to Mr. Williams on my behalf. She hesitated, looked from the Reverend to me, and then said, "Isn't that kind of the Reverend?"

Kind is not the word I would have used for it. Meddlesome maybe. Annoying. A pain . . .

He began telling us about other girls he'd sent to the Asylum. 3 from over to Eddyville. Another from Arcadia. 4 — all from the same family — from Sargent. Then he promised to get the note out immediately.

Irritating, irksome, plaguey, a pest, a bother. Father loved to drill me on synonyms. Said knowing them would help make my conversation and writing lively. I was about to say one of them out loud when Miss Kizer cleared her throat and said she hoped I didn't mind her speaking to the Reverend about my situation.

"When the righteous cry for help," the Reverend stated, "the Lord hears and delivers them out of all their troubles. That is from Psalms and I think it very true." He said all this while looking at Miss Kizer, so I wasn't sure whose troubles he was talking about.

The next moment Miss Kizer was handing me a platter of griddle cakes — the Reverend is very partial to them — and urging me to eat as many as I could. A change of subject, as usual. I took one but didn't do more than cut it into smaller and smaller pieces with my fork. The Reverend's letter would be sent out today and in a few weeks I would be sent out too.

That was when Miss Kizer began talking about the Bocks.

Seems Mr. Bock got very "ill" Wednesday night and hasn't left bed since. Miss Kizer added solemnly that Mrs. Bock's having trouble doing the laundry she takes in.

Then Miss Kizer said she was going to bake for the family. Not so much for the adults, she was quick to point out. She was doing it for the children. Miss Kizer's face took on a stern expression. "I don't approve of his behavior, mind you. But it is my Christian duty to help the less fortunate."

What about me? I wondered. Isn't part of your Christian duty to help me?

Miss Kizer went on talking about the Bocks. All I could think was that I needed to get out of there before I said something very un-Christian. So I blurted out that I would go help Mrs. Bock with the laundry.

Miss Kizer looked surprised, then doubtful, then said no. And repeated no several times. Mrs. Bock is a good woman, Miss Kizer went on, and she is burdened just now, but that Mr. Bock . . . She stopped there, as if more talk about Mr. Bock would make him appear at her shoulder. "I'm concerned about your safety, if I must be frank about it."

I protested. Told her I was stronger than she thought and could run as fast as any boy my age or older.

Miss Kizer was about to say something, but hesitated and then looked to Reverend Lauter for guidance. His mouth opened, but my tongue worked faster this time. It's my Christian duty to help her, I told them. I rummaged through my brain for a good Bible quote but couldn't remember a single line. So I tacked on a fib in its place. "I promised Father I would help others."

That seemed to do it. There was more talk, many cautions about Mr. Bock, and several warnings not to exhaust myself. Eventually, I managed to move away from the table and head upstairs to get ready to leave.

"They admire such industry at the Girls Asylum," the Reverend called after me. He said he'd mention it in his letter to Mr. Williams.

Thought writing this would help me relax. But every time I think that my "industry" is going to be used to send me away from Father I begin shaking all over. Maybe scrubbing dirty clothes will help!

LATER AT NIGHT

Mrs. Bock looked startled when she saw me at the door. The temperature had dropped to near freezing, so she got me inside and the door closed before I could say much more than good morning. When I finally explained why I'd come, she looked uneasy and told me that was very kind but that she could manage.

I said I didn't mind, speaking loudly to be heard over the shouts of the 7-year-old twins, Huey and Jason. "I help Miss

Kizer all the time and I heard about Mr. Bock. That he isn't, you know, feeling well."

Mrs. Bock's face clouded with annoyance and I thought for a second she might bite my head off. Mrs. Bock is very tall — nearly 6 feet tall if I had to guess — and she looks even bigger when she's unhappy. A loud snort came from the next room and then Mr. Bock commenced snoring loudly. What Father would call "sawing logs." Mrs. Bock glanced in his direction and any anger she had disappeared.

Said again that I'd like to help and that I knew I could do a good job. Miss Kizer says the linens have never been as clean as when I do them. And that I found cleaning very peaceful and relaxing.

Mrs. Bock's lips twitched ever so slightly when I said that. Almost as if she wanted to give up a smile. "Well, Sarah Jane," she said, gesturing toward the mounds of laundry against a wall. "If it is peace and relaxation you want, we have piles of it here."

Once I'd found a place for my cloak and bonnet, Mrs. Bock explained what needed to be done and we commenced to work. Because it was so cold outside, everything had to be done in the tiny front room, including the drying. Which meant the clotheslines stretched back and forth from one side of the room to the other and made for a tight fit.

Mrs. Bock already had some clothes soaking in a tub of steaming hot water with lye soap in it. She ran the clothes around the tub with a long stick, then scrubbed them on a washboard. I rinsed them in cold water, squeezed them tight, and hung them over a line.

The room was stifling hot, what with the cook stove blazing away to heat up more pots of water. After 15 minutes of work my dress was soaked with perspiration and I felt light-headed. Mrs. Bock looked the same as I felt, so I made myself continue working.

Meanwhile, Huey and Jason were all over the room — playing hide-and-seek behind the clothes, drawing pictures in the dirt floor with a stick, singing parts of songs. The baby slept for a while, then woke up crying, so Mrs. Bock said we should rest while she nursed her.

Just then Huey and Jason started play-shooting each other. I could see the noise was getting to Mrs. Bock, and I know it was getting to me! So I decided to distract them. It happened by mistake mostly. When Huey was crouching in the corner hiding, I got Jason's attention and told him I needed his help getting my rinse tub outside so I could dump out the dirty water.

Jason agreed and we each took a handle and we lugged the tub out the door and tipped it over. Then I told Jason to fill it half full at the town pump. Huey had followed and wanted to continue the gunfight but I told him Jason was doing something important for me.

When Huey heard this he wanted to help too, but Jason

didn't want him to. They would have argued about this forever, but I said firmly, "Jason can carry the tub to the pump, and you can pump the handle."

Before Jason could say no, I said it was the best way and that both of them could carry it back since it would be heavy.

To my surprise, Huey went off after Jason and it all worked almost the way I had suggested. Huey tugged at the tub several times before they got to the pump, and Jason pulled it away saying that carrying was his job. The same little fight happened with the pumping and then they dropped the first load of water and had to do it all over again.

Eventually, they made it back inside with the clean water and I was able to get them to collect some Nebraska coal. Mrs. Bock was back at the washtub by this time, but she took a moment to look up and say she was impressed by how I'd handled the boys.

Said Father had showed me how to get his students to do chores around the school so I didn't have to do them myself.

"Those 2 need that sort of training," she said. "Get little enough help around here as it is."

An idea flickered in my head. Maybe I could move in with the Bocks and help them. Not for money. Just to have a place to stay.

As I said, that idea flickered and then died cold immediately. Mrs. Bock and her children all look pale and their cheekbones stick out sharp. Hardly food enough for themselves, let alone an additional mouth. And then there's this small soddy and Mr. Bock, snoring and snorting away.

SATURDAY, JANUARY 14, 1882

Dear Little Book,

After breakfast, Reverend Lauter went visiting folks in town. Drumming up business for his prayer meeting, I figured. Or maybe searching for other orphans to send to the Asylum. I was about to slip out too but Miss Kizer wanted me to do a turn at churning so we would have fresh butter.

She has been in a very cheerful mood since the Reverend's arrival and today she seemed more so. I suppose because — with his help — she was sure to be rid of me soon. Finished my chore and was about to escape when Miss Kizer asked me to go to Mr. Pelham's store.

She handed me a list and several silver coins, but before I got very far she added, "And see if he has 2 tallow candles. That will help liven up dinner a bit."

The notion of a livened-up dinner put me in a foul, dark mood, I can tell you. I stalked off, taking the main path past several soddys. The fever had been easing lately — no deaths that I can remember in 3 weeks — but only in the past few days have people begun venturing out. A number said hello, though the strain of fighting the fever still showed in their faces.

After settling with Mr. Pelham and pocketing the change, I left his store. Ida had been standing nearby while her father helped me and I hadn't gotten far before she was right there beside me asking if she could help me carry anything.

There were only a few things in the basket: a jar of Seigel's Headache Syrup, a tin of tea, baking soda, a package of pins, 5 pounds of sugar, and the candles. But Ida looked so eager I said she could take the sugar.

We went past Mr. Tilling's bank and the hotel's now-finished tool shed. A maroon sign next to the door proclaimed in gold letters that this was THE FUTURE SITE OF THE GRAND PARADISE HOTEL.

By this time I realized something was odd about Ida. I glanced at her and then it struck me. She wasn't talking. Then I remembered the black diphtheria and asked her if she was feeling okay.

She ignored my question and instead wanted to know if I was going "to that place for orphans."

She started to tell me exactly how and when she'd overheard Miss Kizer and her parents talking, but I stopped abruptly and demanded, "What about the Asylum?"

And did that get Ida started. She said the Asylum didn't sound like much fun, that the girls are sent out 6 days a week to work at a cloth factory, and that they don't get to keep their pay. In the free time left the girls have to study and pray. They do a lot of praying there, according to her mother.

If Miss Kizer had known this, why hadn't she mentioned it to me? One answer was simple. Because I'd hate the notion of going to the Asylum even more than I already do. But I sensed something else besides.

I wanted to know if there was any discussion of Reverend Lauter. I suspected there was more to his recommending me than his sense of Christian duty. If the Asylum was making money on the girls' labor, he might be getting some sort of fee for every new worker he delivered.

"Only that they were looking forward to his preaching. Is that important?"

Not really I told her. We went on down the path some and then another thought came to me. "Why did you want to tell me this anyway?"

She looked shy suddenly and shrugged. Said she didn't know. That she liked talking with me that last time and guessed she didn't want me to leave. She shrugged her shoulders a second time and added she would have said something sooner but she didn't see me about much.

The last time we'd talked was 2 weeks ago and I have to admit I hadn't thought much about Ida since. Too upset with my own problems. So I told Ida I didn't want to leave either and told her why and what had happened over the past few days and how I was hoping to find a way to stay.

We were almost to Miss Kizer's by this time and Ida was

thinking up ways for me to make money. And rejecting them in the same breath. Things like counting money in Mr. Tilling's bank or helping her father in his store. Only Mr. Tilling doesn't let anybody touch the money in his bank but himself. And her papa has her to help him — and he doesn't ever pay her anything!

We came to the back door and I took the sugar from Ida.

"Thanks for trying," I said and I sighed. Like Miss Kizer. "I guess there's nothing for me to do now."

"You can't give up," she said. "You have to keep thinking on it. Something will come to you."

I wasn't sure she was right. I'd been thinking of just about nothing else for days and not one worthwhile idea had entered my empty head. Oh, well, I thought, at least Ida didn't tell me to pray for an answer.

Sunday, January 15, 1882

Dear Little Book,

Went to the prayer meeting and the Gandys' house was fairly packed with familiar faces. The Gandys, the Tillings, and the Hewitts. Mrs. Bock hovered in one of the bedrooms with her baby in her arms and Jason and Huey behind her. Mr. Bock was nowhere in sight.

Several families from places at the edge of town — the Millers and the Gilmers — and from farms farther out on the prairie — the Huftalens, the Gaddises, the Grundys and more had managed to get there too.

That was when I spotted Ida, over on the other side of the room near the Millers. I smiled at her, but before I could go over, Reverend Lauter began talking.

He began by telling how he'd left the neighboring town of Merna and come down the same trail as he always did to get to Broken Bow.

"10 miles, Brothers and Sisters. 10 twisting, empty miles. And with each mile traveled a great weight filled my heart."

He paused here, his face somber. "Such a great weight," he added, glancing down and shaking his head slowly several times. The room was absolutely quiet. Even the babies had hushed.

Then Reverend Lauter surveyed the room, his eyes going from person to person. When he spoke his voice was soft with sadness. "Because I knew that I would soon arrive at a place where friends had been called from this earth. Where other friends lay sick and suffering. Where still others grieved and carried sadness with them every step of the day. And all that came to mind was 'Why? Why this good town? Why these God-fearing people?'"

I was wondering too — Why Father? Why did the black diphtheria have to get him?

"I see their faces," the Reverend went on. "Smiling and happy and with our Almighty Father . . ."

Then it was as if I wasn't there in the Gandys' house. The Reverend's voice faded away to a whisper. The rustle of clothes and creak of the floor boards disappeared. And Father was back in my head. Smiling and teaching another class — not the Iowa class, but exactly which one of the many he'd taught wasn't clear. But I was there again in the back helping a student.

An angel. That's what Ida had called him. Trying to tell us things and make us do good deeds. What good deed did he want me to perform? Maybe I should just ask him.

Reverend Lauter slapped his Bible hard in the palm of his hand then and I jumped a little. Back I was from my memory, in the Gandys' home surrounded by people. My legs felt shaky, but otherwise everything was real. And I'd missed my chance to talk to Father.

"The Holy Book promises it to you," Reverend Lauter was saying. "It says 'He who dwells in the shelter of the Most High, who abides in the shadow of the Almighty.' Here in Psalm 91 is your promise. 'For He will deliver you from the deadly pestilence.'"

As Reverend Lauter went on, the people at the Gandys' grew more and more animated. Miss Kizer even gave out with a loud "Praise the Lord" at one spot. Maybe that was the Reverend's power — he could say words that made you forget whatever was troubling you. At least for a while.

Which was when I realized something. Both times Father had appeared to me in a schoolroom and both times I'd been helping him to teach. I can read, write, and do numbers. I'd seen Father teach hundreds of times, so I knew what was expected. I could never hope to be as good as Father, but I could still teach a class tolerably well.

And Broken Bow needed a teacher.

When I thought that, I also shouted out "Praise the Lord" with everybody else.

Before the meeting ended, several hymns were sung and the Reverend talked some more, but I wasn't listening. Father had shown me the way to stay in Broken Bow and I was bursting to tell Ida.

Only there were too many people around and I didn't want anybody to hear my idea right then. So we agreed to meet later by the river where we can talk alone. Until then I am going to think about my idea to teach and all of the ways it might go wrong.

LATER

Got to the river before Ida and waited as patiently as I could. The cold had lingered, so I was bundled up tight against the icy, damp wind.

Johnnie Hatter's place was some 200 feet downriver, at a sharp bend where a mess of big rocks spilled out of the bank. Every so often the wind would die down and I could hear his rambling, singsong voice come floating by. The thought that he might pop out of his cave and spot me sent a shiver up my spine, so I slunk back behind a bush.

"Did he talk to you?" a voice asked in my ear.

I jumped and started sputtering, "Ida Pelham, do you always have to . . . to . . . to sneak up . . . on people?!"

Which started Ida into apologizing again for startling me. Eventually, we both calmed down, and I told her what had happened during the prayer meeting. About seeing Father again in a classroom and knowing I could teach too.

Ida whooped very loudly when I told her this. Which made me glad I hadn't said anything to her right at the prayer meeting. "That means you'd be my teacher," she said. Suddenly her smile faded. "But you're not a teacher," she said. "And you're on the young side too."

I told her I didn't think I needed a certificate to teach in Nebraska. I said that I'm close enough to the right age. That's why I wanted to talk to her in private first.

Told Ida about Father getting a copy of the state teaching rules before he'd tried to get a job here in Nebraska and how he had read parts of it out loud to me. I hadn't paid much attention at the time so I wanted to go over the rules one more time. Only I couldn't find Father's copy anywhere and since Ida's father was on the school board, I was hoping he might have the pamphlet.

Of course we couldn't just ask him flat out because then he

would want to know why I needed it. Which set Ida to thinking. I knew she was thinking because her eyes had a distant look to them and she kept muttering to herself. Finally, her face lit up in triumph. Her mama would be cooking in the main room and Timothy would be there too, since he rarely left her side. "If we're lucky, Papa's with them reading a newspaper. His desk is in the other room. Keep them occupied while I look through it, okay?"

This all seemed like a great adventure to Ida, judging by the excited tone of her voice. But I have to tell you, Little Book, I was very nervous. I was thinking about this and about wanting to be a teacher so I could stay in Broken Bow, but when we went in the door to Ida's house, every thought left my head and I stopped short. Along with the rest of Ida's family, Mr. and Mrs. Gaddis were sitting at the table. As if waiting for me to arrive.

Ida froze too. Mr. Gaddis is average height, but he is strong looking and always seems impatient. Even when visiting. He is also the richest person in all of Broken Bow, and is known for his tough dealings. Mr. and Mrs. Gaddis, Ida's father, mother, and brother all turned to look at us.

Ida's papa told her to close the door against the cold and say a proper hello to their visitors.

"Hello, Mr. and Mrs. Gaddis," Ida replied, closing the door behind us. I followed with my own whispered, "Hello, Mr. and Mrs. Gaddis."

Mrs. Gaddis smiled up at us, Mr. Gaddis less so. Ida's parents must have thought something odd was going on. Both were staring at us with furrowed brows.

Ida recovered first and began saying that we had liked Reverend Lauter's sermon and were just saying how it was nice to know that everybody who died was waiting for us in heaven.

Then she turned to me and said, "Right, Sarah Jane?"

All I could do was nod yes, because I was feeling very selfish. I hadn't really thought much about Father since I'd decided on being a teacher. Hadn't even paused a moment to thank him for the idea. All I'd done was worry about how I'd convince everybody to let me teach.

An awkward moment followed with Mrs. Gaddis saying that what the Reverend had said was true. Mr. Gaddis studied the inside of his cup of coffee, while Mr. Pelham nodded solemnly and exchanged glances with Mrs. Pelham. The only one who didn't react was Ida's little brother. He saw that his parents were distracted and grabbed another ginger snap.

Ida's mother cleared her throat and suggested that Ida make herself and me a cup of tea, but Ida said we couldn't because we were going for a walk.

Ida said she had to get some gloves from the other room and left me alone with the adults. Which was not the bad part. Before she ducked through the curtain that separated the rooms, she said, "Oh, Papa. Sarah Jane had a question to ask you."

I wanted to strangle her for saying that.

I managed a little smile and said it wasn't important. But Mr. Pelham said no question is too small.

Everybody was now waiting for me to say something. Mr. Gaddis's chair creaked loudly as he sat back, his head tilted in my direction. Even Ida's brother had stopped munching and was looking at me.

Ida would know what to say and say it as if nothing was the matter. My brain didn't work that way. You could, I instructed myself after what felt like a thousand seconds had passed, ask if any new clothes had come in recently.

But I couldn't bring myself to say the words. Because I knew that I wouldn't sound convincing and Mr. Gaddis and Mr. Pelham — both on the school board — would see right through me and my plan would be rejected.

Then something strange happened. I thought about having to leave Father, about having no say at all in what would happen to me, about missing Ida's friendly chatter, and about being stuck away in the Orphan Girls Asylum and working so other people could get the money. Suddenly a funny tingling sensation began creeping up my neck. From being helpless and wanting to do something — anything! — or explode.

Then a rush of words came tumbling out of my mouth, "I–want–to–teach–school–here–in–Broken–Bow."

The adults all looked at me for the longest time. At last Mr. Pelham asked, "You want to be a teacher? Here?"

I said yes and then explained why I thought I could do the job. At length. How much schooling I'd had, how Father had always taken pains to instruct me on what a teacher had to do to prepare for a class, and more. Fortunately, I must have heard enough when Father had read the rules pamphlet because every time I thought I had run out of things to say, another detail would pop into my head and I'd tell about it.

I must have talked without stopping for 5 or 6 minutes — long enough that I actually began to feel light-headed. Ida slipped back into the room toward the end and when she realized what I was talking about, her face twisted up in an expression that said, "Have you gone completely mad?"

Somewhere along the way I told myself to be confident. Sell yourself, Sarah Jane. Like Mr. Walter Chalmers sells his bitters.

"I know I can do a good job for you," I said. "For the children. If you give me a chance, you won't be sorry at all. I promise."

When I finally stopped, the adults were still staring at me. Mr. Pelham started to say something about it being an interesting idea, but stopped and looked over at Mr. Gaddis.

"Teaching a school is not child's play," Mr. Gaddis said. His voice had an unsympathetic rumble to it.

"I am not a child," I stated. I had raised my voice a little — to show I meant what I said — but I was careful not to go too far. "I'm old enough to teach in Nebraska. Father told me so when he read the state regulations." Since I would be 14 for a few months more, and since Nebraska wants its teachers to be at least 16, this was a definite lie. But I knew I'd have to say something about my age, so why not get past it and move on. I also added that Father said I had enough book learning to do a good job of teaching too.

Mrs. Pelham said something about the Asylum, but I told her I never really agreed and that Miss Kizer decided that on her own.

Mr. Pelham's face had scrunched up some and was hard to read. Might have been thoughtful, might have been downright annoyed. Meanwhile, Mr. Gaddis was shaking his head back and forth and muttering, "No, no. Out of the question. No."

I felt my energy and determination leaving me. Don't give up, I told myself. You have to fight for this.

"Oh, Mama, Sarah Jane would make the best teacher ever." Ida took a few quick steps and was standing next to her mama. She went on saying I know a lot about books and poems. And reminded her papa about how fast I added up things in the store. Faster than even he and in my head. Besides, he said himself that we need a teacher now. Telling him how he said that just the other day when Timothy couldn't count to 20 without making a mistake.

Timothy blurted out that he could too count to 20 and started in saying his numbers.

Ida's father said that the adults there did not need a lecture on what Broken Bow needed. She said something to her father and he said something back. Timothy was still counting, so it all got to be pretty confusing.

Say something in your own defense, the voice in my head commanded. "I can do the job, Mrs. Pelham." I had decided to speak to her because it would be easier than having to look into Mr. Gaddis's doubting eyes. Still my words sounded weak even to me. "I was always helping students and Father let me teach lessons sometimes." And then another detail from the pamphlet came to me. A rule that said if a school district did not already have a teacher, the board was required by law to hire any person who met the basic state requirements. "You have to give me a chance," I added with more confidence. And I shifted my look to Mr. Gaddis. "It's in the Nebraska teaching rules. Father told me about it."

Mr. Gaddis's face took on a deep, maroon color and his eyes seemed to shimmer with anger.

Mrs. Pelham wanted to know if there was such a rule, and Mr. Pelham nodded yes. Ida could not let it end there, of course. In a triumphant voice she announced, "If Sarah Jane says there's such a rule, there is."

Mr. Gaddis was about to say something, and I braced myself for some harsh words. But Mrs. Gaddis interrupted him with a gentle touch of his wrist. She can speak English as well as I can, and with hardly any accent, but she spoke to him in German this time. I had no idea what she was telling him, but I think she was trying to calm him down.

After a brief conversation — when they started, Mr. Gaddis's speech was clipped and angry, but as they went back and forth his voice softened — Mr. Gaddis cleared his throat. Saying Mrs. Gaddis felt — he glanced and nodded at her — that we should at least confer with the rest of the school board about my request. Out of respect for Father and his opinion about my abilities. He stopped and added in a stern tone that, mind us, he is not in favor of giving me the position, rule or no rule. But the board should consider it.

He turned and began talking to Mr. Pelham, asking if he thought a school board meeting could be called that day or the next. I took it that I had been dismissed. Which was fine with me. Said thank you and good-bye, but nobody paid me much mind. Then I was outside with Ida.

"Guess you won't be needing this," Ida said, patting her cloak waist-high where she'd hidden the pamphlet.

"Guess not," I replied. "My idea is out and there's no taking it back now."

She said it was so strange. She was in the other room and heard us all talking, but she didn't know about what. But when she came back in and heard, she just couldn't believe her ears. And why did I do that anyway?

I didn't know. I shrugged my shoulders. I guess you could say I felt "the call upon me."

MONDAY, JANUARY 16, 1882

Dear Little Book,

Woke to find a light snow falling. Usually, I love to watch snow coming down and turning everything white, but today I was too fidgety to enjoy it. When we said good-bye yesterday I made Ida promise to tell me the second she knew what the school board had decided, good or bad. But no word from Ida so far.

Naturally, I worried that Miss Kizer or the Reverend would learn about my plan — either from neighbors or from my eyes — and put a stop to it. I needn't have worried. All during breakfast they discussed the snow, which had begun to come down harder. "The wind is biting hard," the Reverend said. "I believe you are correct, Sister Kizer. The real winter is here at last."

Miss Kizer smiled at this and her cheeks pinked up. She didn't have that haunted look to her eyes. She is sweet on him, I realized, though I guess I should have seen it all along. Whenever she talked about the Reverend, Miss Kizer always seemed more lively and less nervous.

The whole notion of Miss Kizer and Reverend Lauter bothered me. Can't say why exactly. The Reverend didn't seem to pay a lot of attention to Miss Kizer — at least not the romantic kind. I remembered the way his eyes looked the night I first met him. Mesmerizing. I wondered if Miss Kizer had misunderstood one of his looks.

Grace didn't help any. She seemed to be staring at me all day. As if she'd heard about my secret even though no one has come visiting and no one has gone out.

Finished my few chores and came up to my room. Hoping Ida will show up before my nervousness has me shaking all over. At one point, I even stood up next to my bed and practiced talking to a make-believe class. "Class, please pay attention," I began. But it didn't sound right. Too high-pitched and nervous. In a lower tone, I said, "Class, stop talking and take out your readers." No, no, no. Much too severe sounding.

Then I just repeated the word "class" over and over again — each a shade different from the last — until I heard one that sounded right. Did Father ever go through this? He always sounded so calm and relaxed in front of his students, it is hard to believe he was ever new and inexperienced.

Then I told my make-believe class that I was going to recite several poems. I was a little more comfortable hearing my voice, but every so often I would picture a room of restless children staring at me and my voice would falter. Once I tried to gesture with my hands to be dramatic — like Father — but felt silly doing so.

Finally, I did a poem by Mrs. Welby and it came out good

and strong. "The twilight hours like birds flew by / As lightly and as free / Ten thousand stars were in the sky / Ten thousand on the sea / For every wave, with dimpled face / That leaped upon the air / Had caught a star in its embrace / and held it trembling there."

"That was splendid!" Reverend Lauter said from the other side of my closed door. A strange, strangled sound escaped me I was so surprised.

"Forgive me for interrupting, Sarah Jane. I couldn't help hearing and I just had to tell you how well you sounded. Really splendid." I felt good hearing that and said thank you. Then he went and ruined it. "They encourage recitations at the Girls Asylum."

Am sitting on my bed as I write this, wishing Ida would show up. Picked up Father's watch and held it in my hands, remembering how he would polish it every Sunday night until it glistened. My mother gave it to him as a wedding present and sometimes I think he saw her face in the shiny metal.

Snow keeps falling and I watch it slowly turn the brown land white, but no sign of Ida.

TUESDAY, JANUARY 17, 1882

Dear Little Book,

Ida never came by. Snow stopped during the night, but the

sky is a dull gray and threatening more snow. News about the school board meeting is sure to reach here today.

Thought to tell Miss Kizer after breakfast, but put it off again. The Reverend was in his room working on his next sermon and Miss Kizer was in the parlor writing a long letter to her sister. I do not want to disturb the peaceful feeling any.

Later in the morning, there was a *thump-thump* on the back stairs and a loud rap on the kitchen door. I rushed to answer the door and was relieved to see Ida standing there. In a whisper she told me Mr. Gaddis wanted to see me at her house.

I was relieved knowing I wouldn't have to face Miss Kizer just yet. Then I thought about Mr. Gaddis's stern looks on Sunday and got nervous all over again.

Got my cloak and bonnet, told Miss Kizer I was taking a walk with Ida, and slipped out, feeling very cowardly. I expected Ida to be bursting with news about the school board vote, but she didn't know a thing.

We walked along in a gloomy silence with me certain I would be rejected. This feeling was reinforced when we got to Ida's. Mr. Gaddis was sitting at the table, his coat, hat, and gloves on. As if he wanted to get this over with quick and then head home.

Ida's papa was in the store helping a customer. Ida's mother said hello and then guided Ida and Timothy out of the kitchen and into the store, pulling the curtain closed as she did.

"I will be brief and to the point, Miss Price," Mr. Gaddis

began. Miss Price? Said that way my name certainly seemed very formal.

He stood up then. Which I was sure meant he was going to reject my idea and walk out. "I have met with all of the school board members and presented your request. As you know, I am not in favor of letting you teach. . . ." And here he listed the many reasons he didn't think I should have the job.

I listened, but it wasn't easy because an angry feeling was spreading throughout my brain.

"Well, enough of that," Mr. Gaddis said. "The majority of the board — over my strong objections and the objections of 2 others — has decided, Miss Price, to let you teach the children of Broken Bow."

For some reason, I expected to have the news delivered in a more dramatic way. Like Mr. Walter Chalmers talking about his Old Time Bitters. But Mr. Gaddis just said it flat out, then headed toward the curtain leading to the store.

From Mr. Pelham's store Ida gave an excited whoop in celebration. All I could think was that I'd done it. I'd found a way to stay. I wasn't getting shipped off to the Orphan Girls Asylum. "Thank you, Mr. Gaddis," I said.

"Don't thank me," he said coldly. "It's the others that have faith in you, Miss Price. Don't disappoint them."

Then Mr. Gaddis said he had to finish up some business with Mr. Pelham and afterward he wanted to show me the schoolhouse. Seems the soddy he had shown Father way back in September had been rented to three brothers. "Didn't see a reason not to," he explained. "Once your father died, that is. You should get ready now. I want to leave in 20 minutes."

He went through the curtain that led to the store. A moment later, Ida popped back inside, a giant smile on her face.

Told Ida that Mr. Gaddis wanted to show me my school. And, Little Book, I will say that I was smiling as much as Ida when I said "my school."

Ida, of course, wanted to come along, and I said Mr. Gaddis wanted to leave very soon.

"I can be ready before spit dries on a hot stove," she said.

Told her I should go alone in case Mr. Gaddis wanted to talk more. Which Ida thought was silly. He could talk all he wanted in front of her, she insisted. She wouldn't even listen or say anything.

I explained that he didn't say I could invite anybody else. And I didn't want to make him angry. Anymore than he already was anyway. "You understand, right?"

She didn't. That was clear by the disappointed look she wore. But finally she said it was all right, but I had to come right back and tell her all about it.

Promised I would as I went out the door. Then I marched back to Miss Kizer's. Not to tell her where I was going, but to write all this down while it is fresh.

LATER

Wrote that last entry in a running scribble that looks like a foreign language backward. If anybody reads it in the future, they will surely need good, thick glasses.

Finished writing, then hurried back to Ida's and just in time too. Mr. Gaddis was saying good-bye to Mr. Pelham when I got there and he turned to me and said, "Climb up, Miss Price, so we can be going."

Mr. Gaddis said my name in a way that clearly meant he was not happy with me. But it also sounded grown-up, which felt nice.

Ida came to the door to say good-bye. She did her best to be cheerful, but I could tell by the sad little wave she gave as we drove off that she wished she were coming along.

I did too. The ride with Mr. Gaddis was a lonely and quiet one. At least from my side of the wagon.

After we left town, Mr. Gaddis started in telling me about the board meeting. I should say meetings, because it took 2 to decide on me. It was not a unanimous vote, according to Mr. Gaddis. Mr. Tilling and Mr. Gilmer sided with Mr. Gaddis. And even some of the members who voted for me weren't 100 percent sure.

Ordinarily, I might have said something in reply, but I didn't think Mr. Gaddis really wanted a discussion. We went out a half mile from town, then turned down a long sloping path and continued another half mile or so.

Next, Mr. Gaddis told me the board would be watching me carefully and that I could be discharged at anytime if I couldn't handle the job. "The Nebraska state rules provide for that possibility," he added. "But I'm sure you know that already."

That is what I expected, but I never thought it would be said so bluntly. Looked hard at Mr. Gaddis, but he was concentrating on getting the horses over a bump in the path and took no notice of me. Brusque is how Father had described him, but I think rude and disagreeable is a much better description.

Think on something else, I instructed myself. Try to remember the way the paths work. This will be my daily walk after all. And even if he — I didn't want to say his name — even if he doesn't like me, I am the teacher for the spring term. I can't forget that.

We passed a small mound of stones that marked a property boundary. Mr. Gaddis explained that the schoolhouse was on this land up a little way. He had sold the land to an Easterner 2 years ago July, but he didn't last. Mr. Gaddis said in a grumble that hardly any of them do. He bought the land back for less and decided to use his house for the school.

Somewhere, way in the back of my head, I could almost hear Father prompting me to say, "That was very generous of you, Mr. Gaddis," because Father always thought it was important to be nice to all school board members, even the ones who didn't like him. But I don't think Mr. Gaddis cared one way or the other what I felt about anything. Besides, he probably thought of me as a greenhorn Easterner too and assumed I'd pack up and leave soon enough.

I have to tell you, Little Book, I almost did leave when we came up and over another hill and I saw my school. There, at the bottom of a tiny hollow, was the most forlorn excuse for a soddy I have ever seen.

It wasn't very big, for starters. Maybe 15 feet by 20 feet. One window to the right of the wood plank door — with several panes of glass broken. When I got a look around the side of the building, I saw that the wall bulged out in places and was braced up by pieces of tree limbs.

"He wasn't a builder, that's for sure," Mr. Gaddis observed sarcastically, as he pushed open the door to reveal a dank, dark interior. I stepped cautiously inside and immediately felt icy drops of water from melting snow hit my neck and trickle down my back. It also smelled of wet and rot.

Mr. Gaddis struck a match and held it up. Aside from a small table, a wood chair, a rusty stove with its stovepipe all collapsed on the floor, and a pile of sticks for kindling, the place was empty. Not even a curtain for the window.

Mr. Gaddis admitted the school wasn't much to look at before dropping the first match and lighting another. "But it's better than nothing."

It is nothing! I screamed. Inside my head, of course. And I might even have said it out loud except I was too shocked to open my mouth. Johnnie Hatter's hole in the riverbank is probably better than this.

Mr. Gaddis tried to make it sound less horrible by suggesting that all it needed was a little airing out and by promising that the school board would have the roof patched, the window and stove fixed, and get some firewood delivered. "The wall will probably need more support," he added. "That man — Tyson was his name. John Tyson — spent most of his time trying to dig a well instead of planting crops or doing repairs."

Mr. Gaddis put out his second match and left the soddy. As soon as I was outside, he pointed off into the distance and told me there was a creek 100 feet beyond the next hill. He also said that the board would provide a bucket and a ladle.

He didn't wait for me to say anything, but turned and went back to his wagon. Stunned, I followed and got on the wagon after giving my school one parting glance. What have I gotten myself into? I wondered, as Mr. Gaddis turned the wagon around and headed back to town.

That was when he told me the rest of the news. I wasn't getting a set pay. Instead, he handed me a slip of paper with the names of 18 eligible students in our district. I was going to be paid one dollar a pupil per month based on the average daily attendance. "Of course, tardy students are considered absent."

Which meant that if it snowed and no one showed up at school for 2 or 3 days, the average daily attendance would drop below 18. And that assumed that all 18 would show up when the weather was good, which usually isn't the case.

"But that's less than half what Father was supposed to make," I said before I could tell myself to be quiet.

He never took his eyes from the narrow path as he explained that Father had a college diploma, a teaching certificate, and years of experience. He also had to support me. For my age and experience, he said the board felt this arrangement was more than fair.

It wasn't really the board. It was him. And I bet he made the others agree before he would hire me. The law didn't say anything about how much — or how little — to pay a teacher!

Don't say a word, Sarah Jane, I cautioned myself. Hold it in even if you will burst as a result. So I did just that. Sat there fuming and in such foul humor that I hardly felt the wet sting as snow began falling.

"Another thing, Miss Price. Because of the fever, no books or supplies were ordered. You'll have to make do as best as you can. Mr. Pelham thinks we'll have them by next fall."

Next fall! He meant after they'd gotten rid of me. Well, I

have Father's books for a start and maybe I could find some others besides. Paper, pencils, and such other supplies were another matter entirely and I was puzzling over this problem as we neared town.

We splashed across a stream and several soddys came into view. Just then Mr. Gaddis started telling me that a teacher has to be aware of her position in a small town like Broken Bow, and that I had to put some distance between me and my students.

I didn't know what he was talking about and my face must have said so because Mr. Gaddis looked annoyed and added, "You are no longer one of the students. You are the teacher and should act like one at all times."

To which I said, "Yes, of course."

"Good," he said. He called to his team to slow and applied the foot brake at the same time. "Here we are now. I'll need to see your daily programme soon to share with the rest of the board. Spring term begins on February 27. A Monday."

We stopped at the back door of Miss Kizer's and I leaped off the wagon as quickly as I could. I was in such a hurry to be away from Mr. Gaddis that I was inside before remembering to report back to Ida.

Found everything quiet and still. That meant Miss Kizer and the Reverend were out visiting. I used this quiet time to write in you, Little Book. I have a feeling it won't be quiet for long.

LATER

Heard a door slam and then a voice came from the parlor, "Sarah Jane, please come in here." It was Miss Kizer, and she knew.

Went in and my mind was racing. Just how angry is she? I wondered. The moment I saw Miss Kizer's eyes — all dark and troubled and disappointed — I knew the answer. Even the way she said, "We need to talk, Sarah Jane," told me she was angry. I was so nervous I didn't even sit down. I think because I wanted to be ready to run away if I had to.

After that she told me how Mrs. Tilling had finally told her my news and how embarrassing it was to be the only person in town not to know. I tried to explain, but Miss Kizer didn't want to hear any of my excuses. She said I should have said something to her out of respect. I can tell you that I felt very guilty too.

Then my mind fastened onto Mrs. Tilling's name. Had they talked much about me — about how old I was? Was Mrs. Tilling right now telling her husband the truth that would undo everything?

"The Girls Asylum is the best place for you," Miss Kizer insisted. "You would be safe there, you would get a good education, you wouldn't have to worry about where you would sleep or get a meal."

"And I'd have to work 6 days a week for it too," I blurted

out angrily. "You should have told me *that* when you were telling me how wonderful a place it was. Ida had to tell me about working in the cloth factory."

Startled is what she was when she realized I'd discovered that and then her eyes darted around nervously. She began to tell me again that it was a fine, Christian place and that Mr. Williams would look after me.

"I don't want Mr. Williams looking out for me at all!" I yelled. Heard thumps on the back steps as the Reverend stamped his feet to get snow off his boots. I did not want to be around to hear him tell me what a great opportunity I would be missing, what a great man Mr. Williams was, or whatever else he might say. "I can look out for myself," I said, lowering my voice and turning to go to my room.

Miss Kizer called after me, saying we needed to talk more about this. That teaching was not what I —

"You're not my mother," I said firmly, glancing around at her. "And you can't tell me what to do either!"

Reverend Lauter entered the parlor as I strode across the room, but I didn't say hello or even look at him. Just kept my head down and got inside my bedroom, closed the door, and tried to forget the hurt look on Miss Kizer's face.

꒰ ꒱

LATER STILL

Threw myself on my bed and waited, expecting Miss Kizer to knock and order me to come out. She might even tell me to pack my things and leave. Or maybe the Reverend would quote from the Bible. Something about a prodigal daughter, if there was any such.

But nobody came and I was left with my thoughts.

And they were spinning around like a whirlwind. I shouldn't have said that — about Miss Kizer not being my mother. Even though it's true, and she shouldn't be bossing me around! The only good thing I could see in it all was that she hadn't said anything about me being too young to teach. Maybe she didn't say anything to Mrs. Tilling.

The wind whipped the snow against my window, rattling it. Miss Kizer and the Reverend had moved into the kitchen and were talking. In voices too low to understand. They weren't discussing what to have for dinner, that much I knew.

I wish Father would appear — so I could ask him what to do about Miss Kizer. Because I really don't want her angry at me. Or how I should handle Mr. Gaddis and that thing he calls a school.

Every time I thought of Mr. Gaddis and how he'd gotten a teacher for a bargain and that he could — and wanted to — fire me at any moment, my blood began to boil. "I'm going to show him," I muttered out loud. "I will. I'll be such a good teacher he'll be sorry."

The sky grew darker as the afternoon wore away. Heard Miss Kizer in the kitchen starting supper. Thought to see if she needed help, but was too embarrassed by what I'd said. Wished she would rap on my door and tell me that I should be peeling potatoes so the Devil wouldn't get me.

The smell of cooking chicken reached me about then and I found myself very hungry. A few minutes later, Miss Kizer announced flatly, "Sarah Jane. Supper will be ready in a few minutes." That was all.

Her voice had lost that sharp edge it had before, but it certainly was not welcoming either.

When I got to the kitchen, I asked if I could do anything and Miss Kizer said to call Reverend Lauter. He was outside fixing the latch to the convenience. She didn't look at me while she said this and her voice was distant and distracted.

Thought to say I was sorry — about saying she wasn't my mother. But then I worried that she might start in all over again about the Orphan Girls Asylum and my teaching, so I decided to put that off a little. Set out the plates, utensils, and napkins, then poked my head out the door to call the Reverend.

That was when I realized something else Mr. Gaddis had done, and I groaned out loud. Miss Kizer asked if something was wrong and I said no.

Because I couldn't tell her. It would just be more proof to her that I was a little girl and needed to be protected and looked after. You see, Little Book, I realized then that I hadn't seen an outhouse near my school. Where, I wondered, were my students and I supposed to pee?

I will bet anything that Mr. Gaddis is at home now very pleased with himself. And I guess I will have to do the best I can with what I've got.

WEDNESDAY, JANUARY 18, 1882

Dear Little Book,

Miss Kizer was very snappy when I came in to help with breakfast. Said do this and do that, but did not smile or say anything else. Not that this surprised me. Supper last night was very quiet with Miss Kizer saying as little as possible and almost nothing to me. At least she hadn't told me to get out of her house.

Reverend Lauter knew what had happened, because his eyes had lost their warmth when he said to me, "I've heard your news, Sarah Jane. I can't say it's the right choice at all." I expected him to add a Bible quote or to begin a lecture, but he didn't. He only added, "I won't tell Mr. Williams about your plans. Not just yet. But I will tell you something. Sister Kizer is extremely disappointed in you."

So meals last night and today went by quietly. Except that

today after breakfast Miss Kizer announced there were chores to do.

I have to say, Little Book, that I did not like the way she said this. More like a command than a request. I almost said I was a boarder and wouldn't do the chores. Ida would have. But I did as ordered without complaint because everything felt uncomfortable already and I didn't want to make it worse.

Then Miss Kizer said I was moving too slowly and I felt that familiar tingling up my back that means I'm getting angry. The next time she scolded me, I said if I cleaned the table any more I would take the color out of the wood and Miss Kizer snapped back, "Cleanliness is next to Godliness and don't you forget it."

This time I did not think before speaking. "I am a paying boarder so why do I have to do chores?" came out and Miss Kizer stopped what she was doing and stared at me. "Because," she said in a low, but firm, voice, "you have a reduced weekly fee." Then she left the room before I could respond.

I went at my work very hard, seeing either Miss Kizer or Mr. Gaddis's face in every dish I washed and scrubbing extra hard.

When I finished up, I went directly to Ida's. Before I could say a word, she demanded to know why I hadn't come back yesterday after Mr. Gaddis dropped me off. Tried to explain — about Mr. Gaddis being mean and having a fight with Miss Kizer. The only thing that got her attention was when I told her

I was being paid less than a regular teacher. Which seemed to win her over.

She was even more sympathetic when I described the condition of my school and downright mad when I told her Mr. Gaddis didn't want me playing with my students and being silly and such.

"That's stupid," Ida declared. "He can't boss you around like that."

"Yes, he can," I said.

She didn't say a thing, I think, because she saw I was really nervous about this. And she knew Mr. Gaddis *could* boss me around. When she spoke again, her voice wasn't so upset. Said we wouldn't be playing when we fixed up the school. We'd be cleaning and moving things.

Told her I'd see, but I had to be careful.

Mrs. Pelham had come in toward the end of this talk, trailed as always by Timothy. He was on the list of students Mr. Gaddis had given me, but I wondered if he would ever leave his mother's side long enough to attend school.

So I asked and she said quite definitely, yes. She glanced and saw the sour look Timothy flashed. "None of that, Mister. You are going to school and you'll learn your letters and numbers. Is that clear?"

Took out the list of names and checked off Ida and Timothy. Then I had a thought. I would visit everybody on my list to introduce myself and find out if they would be coming to school. That way I'd have some idea of my class size — and how much money I would earn.

Ida wanted to come along, of course, but I reminded her about Mr. Gaddis and told her I should do this myself. "I think he's being very mean and stupid," she said, "and you should tell him so."

Mrs. Pelham told Ida to hold her tongue and show respect for her elders. But Ida's eyes were still bright with anger when she turned to me and asked if she could help me get my school ready. To which I said yes and left.

LATER

Ran all the way back to Miss Kizer's and arrived just as she was taking a great black pot from the stove. Wished I could tell her about my day and talk about how I might get my school in order. But of course I couldn't.

And then there was what I'd said about being a paying boarder. Wished I could take that back. "Can I help, Miss Kizer?" I asked.

"I can manage, Sarah Jane," she said a little coldly. There was a space of silence and then she added, "but thank you for offering." This second part came out less annoyed, which was a relief.

Went into the parlor and found the Reverend looking

through his Bible. He looked up and stared at me, his eyes as hard as black rocks. "Good evening, Sarah Jane," he said in an icy tone, then went back to reading before I could answer. He did not get up when I entered, as he had done in the past and he hadn't said "good evening" in his usual, dramatic way.

Waited in my room and finished up my daily programme, which is a plan for what my scholars will do throughout the day. I'm to give it to Mr. Pelham and he'll see that it gets to Mr. Gaddis and the other board members.

I've left the door slightly open so I can hear better if Miss Kizer needs my help. Grace just stopped at the door, looked at me a second, then turned, and pranced off. Feel very much apart and wonder if this is how it will be around here from now on? I am holding Father's watch in my hands and wishing I could see his smile again.

SATURDAY, JANUARY 21, 1882

Dear Little Book,

Things have been very quiet and chilly in the house these past days, so I spent as much time as possible visiting parents and scholars. The Hewitts, Bocks, Millers, Womeldorfs, and Merriwethers all said their children will attend school — so I will have at least 10 students. The Tillings said "No" and wouldn't even talk about it, and the Gilmers are still thinking about it.

Next I headed farther out of town — to Mr. or Mrs. Huftalen's farm some 3 miles out.

Mrs. Bock told me to take the trail out of town, then go right and the Huftalens' farm was "just up a piece." Even with snow on the ground, her directions were fairly easy to follow. In fact, the only trouble I had was that I went over a hill and there was Johnnie Hatter out a ways with a small, furry creature wriggling in his arms. Probably trying to kill dinner, I thought. Which made me hasten my step along, I can tell you.

Up a piece turned out to be 2 long, snowy miles. I was exhausted when I finally reached their farm, my shoes soaked through, and wishing I'd asked Ida to give me a ride. Since neither Mr. or Mrs. Huftalen speaks much English, Carl — who is ten, but is small and looks younger — had to translate English into German back and forth.

Carl was reluctant at first — when I told him why I was there he blurted out, "I'm ta be a farmer. Why do I need readin' 'n writin'!" But then he went ahead and told them who I was and that I was the new teacher for the Broken Bow school.

Mr. and Mrs. — I'm just going to call them that to save time — talked between themselves for a minute or so, then asked how old I was. I told them 16 and smiled confidently. I've said my age is 16 so often these past days that it feels almost true now.

Mr. and Mrs. went back to their conversation. What are

they saying, I asked Carl, who shrugged and said, "Oh, they think you look very young for being 16 and such."

Just then they said something to Carl who asked me what sort of schooling I had. After I answered I asked Carl what was going on, but before he could get much out, his parents had another question for me. It went like this for a long while, with me answering a question now and then, followed by a discussion that Carl never quite got to tell me about.

Somewhere in here, I glanced out the window and noticed a light snow falling. It was very pretty the way it swirled and swooped around.

That's when I thought about the path. An inch or so of snow would completely cover and wipe it out.

I said something to Carl about the snow, but he wasn't much concerned. Maybe he figured if I got lost and died in the snow he could escape school a while longer.

Mr. and Mrs. asked a few more questions, then, very suddenly, they turned, both smiling happily, and Mr. nodded several times and said something directly to me. Carl didn't wait for me to ask for a translation this time. "Father said you're the closest to a real teacher that we have right now. So I'll be there — as long as the chores are done."

After a pause, Carl added, "And he asked if you would like a cookie."

I took the cookie, thanked both Mr. and Mrs. for listening to me, then hurried off into the snow. The path was already beginning to disappear and it had only been snowing for 15 minutes. Still I managed to make my way back to where it widened and was lucky enough to catch a ride to town with a farmer coming in for supplies.

Checked my list again: 1 no, 2 maybes, and 11 yeses. 11 dollars per month so far, which leaves me — after paying Miss Kizer — about $2.60. There are still 4 students on my list, but they all live several miles out and will have to wait for another day.

SUNDAY, JANUARY 22, 1882

Dear Little Book,

Thought to skip the prayer meeting today, I was so tired from yesterday's walking. But decided to go in the end. Mr. Gaddis would be there and I didn't want him thinking poorly of me. A teacher, I have heard, has to be aware of her position in a small town.

Glad I did go. After finding Ida, I was surprised by several of the parents coming up to say again they were happy I would be teaching. One said he had found half of an old *McGuffey Eclectic Reader* and would lend it to me. Jason and Huey asked if I was coming over again soon to help with the washing, but

Mrs. Bock hushed them and said I was a teacher now and to show proper respect.

Felt important and grown up. Then I saw Mr. Gaddis looking in our direction and he was not smiling, let me tell you.

My face flushed and I began edging away from Ida. She didn't know why I was moving away and came to stand next to me again.

Reminded Ida about the warning Mr. Gaddis had given me about acting like a teacher. Ida looked confused. Then she spotted Mr. Gaddis and immediately scowled — the most fearsome one I have ever seen at a prayer meeting. "He doesn't scare me," she said in a determined whisper. She moved right next to me again.

I started moving away from her again and when she saw this she seemed doubly annoyed. At him and me!

"Sarah Jane . . ."

"Please," I said, glancing over toward Mr. Gaddis who was talking with Mr. Tilling. Another one who was not keen to have me teach.

I was saved when Reverend Lauter began the meeting. Some few paces to my right was Miss Kizer, whose face had lost its tight, pained look and now seemed relaxed. Almost tranquil. Was it being at prayer meeting that had done that for her, or was it Reverend Lauter?

The meeting was very spirited and the Reverend gave a lively talk about overcoming the hardships of life and building something good and lasting out of nothing. Everybody in Broken Bow knows about hardship and building something from nothing and most heads were nodding in agreement.

"Oh, but be aware, Brothers and Sisters. Be aware of false pride in your achievements. Of wanting more than your neighbors. Of placing yourself above others. Remember!" Here he paused and held his Bible high in the air with his right hand so that the gold lettering on the front sparkled. "Remember, the Lord has chastised mighty empires for their arrogance. The Egyptians felt His wrath. The power of the Babylonians crumbled and disappeared. And Obadiah tells us of his warning to the Edomites: 'The pride of your heart has deceived you. . . . Though you soar aloft like the eagle, though your nest is set among the stars, thence I will bring you down, says the Lord.'"

A murmur of approval circled the gathering, though I felt very strange indeed at that moment. Was I imagining things or had Reverend Lauter looked directly at me while he said those words?

The Reverend went on to describe in detail how these prideful nations had fallen, then moved quickly to the rewards of humility and good, honest work.

Good, honest work. That phrase echoed in my head several

times, I think because that's all I really wanted to do. Yet, here were Mr. Gaddis, Mr. Tilling, Reverend Lauter, and Miss Kizer all trying to stop me from doing so. Too young and inexperienced they all said, even though I've been in classrooms all of my life. Why couldn't they at least let me try?

Suddenly I needed a fast-and-true friend. So as soon as Reverend Lauter finished his preaching I turned to Ida and said, "Want to see the schoolhouse tomorrow?"

"About time," she said with a trace of anger. Then her lips curled into a smile. "We need to get working on it, don't we, Teach?"

"Ida!" I said, looking around quickly to see if anybody had heard. And when I turned back she said, "You know, Sarah Jane, you worry too much."

MONDAY, JANUARY 23, 1882

Dear Little Book,

Bitter cold and windy. Put together some of the books for my school in a satchel, but decided to visit Father before going to Ida's. At first I was a little confused at the cemetery because I hadn't been there in a while and didn't immediately find Father's grave. Which is near the middle, but even knowing that didn't help.

Everything was white with the recent snow, the ground

and wood crosses alike. And the mound of dirt at his grave had collapsed; it blended in with all the others.

But I found him, of course. Told him that I missed him, told him about my past few days and how some people were against me. Then I asked him why he hadn't appeared again. No, Little Book, I did not expect an answer as I stood there holding my cloak closed tight against the biting cold. But I wanted to let Father know I was lonely and still needed him.

Then I went to Ida's and we set off on her horse, Henry, Ida in front and me hanging on behind her as best as I could. Ida knew where Mr. Tyson had had his place and had no trouble finding my school. Thought I heard Johnnie Hatter when we were halfway there, but Ida got Henry moving fast, so I never actually saw him.

When we arrived at my schoolhouse, Ida did not even get off Henry for the longest time. She just sat and stared at the building. All she said was, "Oh, Sarah Jane, I am so sorry."

Eventually we set to work, though we kept our cloaks on because it was so miserably icy inside the school. Ida helped me take everything out of the building, including the kindling. Found a broom with a broken handle and swept the dirt and 2 dead voles out of the room. We put the table, which has strong legs, and the chair back in. That will be where I sit.

Ida wondered what we were going to use for seats. I didn't know, of course. I didn't know what I was going to do with any of it„ really. All I knew was that I wasn't going to let Mr. Gaddis win. I wasn't going to be like the other greenhorns who came and went and were forgotten.

Sometime later, Mr. Bock arrived with a wagon load of firewood and chips. With classes now scheduled to begin, everyone in Broken Bow had been given a school assessment, an amount of money each one owed to keep the school — me! — operating for the 3 months we would be in session.

Since many people don't have ready cash, they pay in kind. Mostly in wood and cow chips for the stove. Mr. Bock didn't even have extra chips, so he paid by collecting everything and bringing it here in one of Mr. Pelham's wagons. He rolled a great 8-foot-long limb off the wagon and stood up, his face already a livid red from the exertion.

Ida asked Mr. Bock if he was going to cut it.

"No ax," he said in his thick accent. "The high and mighty one. He ordered me to bring wood and that's what I do. I have other work to do."

His still, he means, but it wouldn't do to say this. I asked what I was supposed to do with it. It won't fit in the stove.

Mr. Bock rolled another log off and cursed when a broken branch jabbed him in the thigh. "I will bring an ax next time and you will chop," he said, rubbing at the bruised spot. "If you have bad boys in class — like those Hewitt boys, Fred and Ed — have them chop. And if their daddy complains, I would say it is an . . . what is the word? Oh, yes, is an educational experience. Like counting numbers."

Which wasn't a bad idea at all. Ida agreed, though she said she'd have bad girls chop also. We left a little after because of the cold, got confused on the way back, but not lost. At one point, Ida wondered if the board would get me a new school if this one burned down. "By accident, of course," she said quickly.

Fire would solve a lot of that building's problems. But I doubt if I'd get another school. At least not until another Easterner abandons his claim.

WEDNESDAY, FEBRUARY 1, 1882

Dear Little Book,

26 days to go before school opens. I am so nervous and yet I can't wait for the first day! Why can't the month hurry up and be done! Can hardly sit still during the day or sleep at night.

TUESDAY, FEBRUARY 7, 1882

Dear Little Book,

I am sorry for ignoring you so many days. I have gone to my school every day since I wrote in you last, bringing a few books each time. Ida has come along most times and is very helpful.

Mr. Bock has made a few improvements to my school too. He reassembled the stove pipe, repaired the window, and filled up the bigger cracks in the ceiling with new chunks of sod. Today he brought in several long pieces of timber to hold up the side, but I can't say it looked any stronger.

"Here you go, Miss," Mr. Bock said when he was about to leave. He handed me an ax, pail, and tin ladle. "From the generous school board."

Ida's mother had sent along some curtains and a metal rod for my window. We used the back of the ax to drive 2 long nails into the sod, then hung the rod on them.

Next we hung up an American flag the saloon keeper lent me. He'd heard from Mr. Bock what the schoolhouse was like and called me over one day. "It's dirty, full of holes, and don't look like much," he'd said, handing me the flag. "But it went through the war with me from Bull Run to Appomattox, so you take care of it, hear?"

Thought about Father as we put it up on the back wall. Now when my scholars do their Opening Exercise it will be to a flag with a real history. The saloon keeper also said he'd send along some empty wood boxes to use as seats, but they haven't arrived yet.

We pinned up pictures from magazines, little maps I'd cut from one of Father's books, and some colored ribbons.

"It looks nice," said Ida when our work was finished. "Cheerful."

"I'm not sure this place will ever look cheerful, Ida. But it looks better."

Then in a very prim and proper voice, Ida added, "It does indeed look respectable, Miss Price." We both managed to laugh out loud at that. But I reined mine in quick.

A voice inside my head was wondering how loud a teacher should laugh. Would Mr. Gaddis think I hadn't kept a proper distance between myself and a student? Which I knew was silly. My being the teacher didn't change the fact that Ida had said something funny just when we needed it. Still, I glanced nervously out the window to see if Mr. Gaddis was near.

Went back to Miss Kizer's late in the afternoon. No one about but in the kitchen I found an oil lamp and a piece of apple pie on a dish on the side table. A note from Miss Kizer tucked underneath said:

Dear Sarah Jane,
Made this pie from apples Mrs. Pelham sent over. I also
heard that your school is dark and cheerless . . .

That surprised me since I didn't think she cared much about it.

. . . and I thought this lamp might be useful. Also, I brought these pages of leaves from the East. They might look nice for the walls and might also help your students to tell the difference between an oak and a maple and a sumac, which is an important skill even out here on the prairie.
Miss Kizer

I smiled at that. Trust Miss Kizer to be ever practical.

The 5 large pages were wrapped in newspaper and carefully tied with white string. When I finally got the package open I found sheets of heavy paper filled with leaves, each leaf glued down perfectly. Below each leaf, precise, neat handwriting, unmistakably Miss Kizer's, told its name.

Looked at the newspaper and saw the date, August 2, 1877, at the top.

My stomach let me know why I'd come to the kitchen then, so I retied the package as carefully as I knew how and ate the slice of pie that had been left for me. Came back to my room to write this and think about what Miss Kizer's gifts might mean.

MONDAY, FEBRUARY 13, 1882

Dear Little Book,

Been sick these past days. No, not with the black diphtheria, thank the Lord. Felt tired and sneezed a lot some days back, then a fever set in. This all in one long, trying night. By the next day I was all used up and had a dreadful pain in my left ear. Dr. Merriwether studied my throat, eyes, ears, and nose in a very serious way, then instructed me to stay in bed 5 days.

Said I had to get my school ready, but Miss Kizer fussed and scolded and tended to me. Which was more than kind, considering what I'd said to her, and the fact that 2 men from the railroad arrived and she had them, the Reverend, and me to look after on her own. And when I apologized for not being able to help out, she just waved my worry away. "I've run this house by myself when it was packed full, so don't you fret on it."

I did fret about my school, of course. Didn't have much else to do. And more than once I thought to apologize to Miss Kizer about our fight, only I never found the right words. Yesterday — my 4th day in bed — was well enough to sit up.

Miss Kizer came in and began straightening things here and there.

"About what I said, Miss Kizer," I began. "About you not being my mother . . ."

"Never you mind that. You were upset and so was I. We all say things we shouldn't at those times." She said this in a very matter-of-fact way. Was that anger I heard in her voice, or was it just her way to get beyond an unpleasant subject and back to normal?

I said I should have told her about the teaching. Even if she wasn't going to help me. And I apologized.

She was at the door and about to leave, but she paused a moment. "Sarah Jane, you've made up your mind about teaching here and so has the school board. It's settled and that's that, as far as I'm concerned. And about what you said, it was only the truth, after all. Now, be still a while and I'll bring you some warm milk."

She ducked out the door before I could say, "But we need to talk more about this."

FRIDAY, FEBRUARY 17, 1882

Dear Little Book,

What a week, Little Book. Felt better on Monday — knew I was past my sickness because I woke up impatient to be at my school. Only Miss Kizer wouldn't let me do more than get dressed and walk around the house. Ida was busy on Tuesday, then rain fell for 2 days straight. So it wasn't until today that I could get there with her.

Saloon keeper's boxes had arrived and were set out in neat rows. By Mr. Bock, I assume. Each box had a picture of a big, angry black dog on it and the words THE GATZWEILER BEER COMPANY, ST. PAUL, NEBRASKA. Odd, but they will do as seats.

Stood next to my desk to see what my room was like. Even with the lamp lit, it was all a little sad looking.

Started thinking about one of Father's schools in Pennsylvania. It was made of red brick with shutters on all 6 windows and a beautiful bell tower above the front door. And a convenience just around the side!

I could still see that school clearly, the shiny, new desks, each with an inkwell; a blackboard covering the entire side wall; and a big, stout pot-bellied stove in the corner. And the smells — of fresh paint, chalk, and sweet wood smoke. That was what a school should look and smell like, I thought.

Then I was back inside Mr. Tyson's soddy. What would Father — But I stopped that question before it was even asked. This was *my* school and I'd just have to stop complaining and learn to live with it.

Spent the rest of the time chopping wood, first me and then Ida. We did this inside so we would be out of the wind. After we'd gotten a few pieces cut, I started a fire in the stove. It didn't give off much heat, but at least the snap and crackle of the burning kindling was comforting.

SUNDAY, FEBRUARY 26, 1882

Dear Little Book,

Reverend Lauter gave a very heated talk today, filled with avenging armies and flashing swords for all sinners. Must confess to not listening carefully. Kept thinking about tomorrow — my first day teaching my students in my school.

Back in my room I took up Father's watch, set it to the correct time, and wound it. I will need the watch to follow my daily programme. Soon its familiar ticking filled the room, almost like the beating of a heart.

Monday, February 27, 1882

Dear Little Book,

Slept very little, I was so nervous. Made myself breakfast, then bundled up for my walk to school. Arrived alone and scared, but soon had a comforting fire burning. Before leaving I grabbed you, Little Book, and plan to add to you when there is time during the day. Such as right now. But I expect to be very busy once my scholars start arriving.

Later in the Morning

Oh, what a morning! I will set it down here, but wish I could forget. School is scheduled to start at 9 o'clock, but I began looking out for students at 8:30, and when I didn't see any eager faces approaching I wondered if everybody had changed their minds. A silly thought.

Oh, how I wish Father were here to reassure me and quiet my jumpy stomach and say just the right thing. Once, in Pennsylvania, he and I were alone before the first day of classes began. "Every year a new beginning," he said. "Children will walk in here today who can't read or even count. By the end of the session they'll have more in their heads than they ever dreamed of. That's one of the rewards of teaching, Sarah Jane. Passing on these skills."

My reward isn't so lofty. I am teaching so I can earn money to stay in Broken Bow.

After a while I heard 2 voices and soon 2 children came walking over the hill. It was Jason and Huey, and they were arguing over whose turn it was to carry their lunch bucket. Father's pocket watch said there was still 20 minutes until class officially began.

Before either boy reached the school, Ida came riding up, her brother, Timothy, bouncing along behind her. As they neared the soddy, Timothy leaped from Henry and dashed into the school, shouting that he was the first one ever in Broken Bow's school!

Ida frowned at him and then at me. She was clearly in a grumpy mood. From not being able to accompany me to school? She got off Henry and smacked the horse on the rump. "Go home, Henry." And he did, trotting past Jason and Huey and another student who had appeared up the path a way.

I heaved a sigh of relief. At least some scholars would show up.

Ida went inside and I hurried the Bock boys in after her and then Charles Denning, who is 15 or 16 and more than a head taller than me. Next, a wagon pulled up outside. 3 children varying in age from 5 to 14, I think, jumped down. Without a word, the driver tipped his hat in my direction and departed.

Greeted the children as they approached me, told them I was their teacher, and gave them my name. I assumed these were the Pospisil children, Nora, Alfred, and Alrah. They lived south of town beyond walking distance, so I hadn't gotten out to their farm to introduce myself. The oldest, Nora, nodded and said something to me in German, and then introduced herself and her sister and little brother.

Suggested they go inside and find seats, but Alfred didn't seem to understand, so I pointed and said, "Go. Inside. Seats." Nora still looked confused, but she did herd Alrah and Alfred through the door.

The pocket watch said there was still 10 minutes before class was to start. With 8 students already inside and waiting for me to begin, those 10 minutes seemed like a very long time indeed.

A bell, I told myself. I should have a bell to signal when school is to begin. Like the one Father had in Pennsylvania. Another silly thought. I should have books, chalk, pencils, paper and a blackboard too but that wasn't likely anytime soon. What chance would I ever have of getting a bell?

The Hewitt boys strolled up, laughing and shoving each other. "Morning, Teach," Edwin said, much to the amusement of his brother.

"Find a place and sit down, please," I said in an even, pleasant voice. Always set a good example, Father had instructed me more than once. Which is why I said "please" very distinctly.

"Yes, Ma'am," Fred replied, dragging out the ma'am for as long as he could to the delight of Edwin.

I ignored them, mostly because I had no idea what I should say and I didn't want to make the situation worse.

Now what? I wondered, glancing inside. The students were all seated and waiting for me to begin. Fred and Edwin began arguing, and little Alfred Pospisil, who is 5 if I understood Nora correctly, yawned in a very loud manner and looked about to nod off.

Still a few minutes to go, I noticed. I'll just stay out here to greet — But then I thought, Sarah Jane Price, you are standing out here because you are afraid of going in *there*. Either start teaching or start packing. Took one last glance around, then turned and went inside to face my class, pulling the door closed to keep out the icy gusts that swept down into the hollow.

"While we wait —" My voice broke from nervousness and I had to clear my throat before I could continue. "Wait for the other children, I'd like one of you to read a passage from the Bible. Who would like to try? Raise your hand, please."

Well, I'd gotten the question out and it hadn't sounded horrible. And several hands were in the air. Good, I thought, at least a few can read, which will make my work a little easier.

Ida's hand was up, but she wasn't waving it back and forth to get my attention like the others and didn't look particularly eager either. So I called on her.

Ida looked surprised, but leaped up and hurried to my desk, where I had 3 Bibles. "Old Testament or New?" she asked. "And from which book? The Old has all of those begats and begits, but I think it sounds prettier when you get to the stories, don't you, Sarah Jane?"

I told her it was her choice, then I leaned close to her ear and added in a whisper, "Remember, it's Miss Price in here, okay?"

"Oh," she said, looking embarrassed. "Sorry. Miss Price."

As she read, other children arrived — Carl Huftalen sporting a mighty scowl, Willa Miller, the Womeldorfs' two girls, Henrietta, who was 12, and her 4-year-old sister, Mary. Heard running feet and then Andy Merriwether burst into the room, apologizing in a gasping voice.

15 scholars so far. Three were absent and probably would never show up — as long as I was the teacher. But 15 meant I would make enough to pay Miss Kizer.

It wasn't yet 9 o'clock, but I couldn't wait any longer. I had

Ida sit down and then I began the Opening Exercise. Which took longer than my scheduled 5 minutes because half my students did not know the words to "The Star-Spangled Banner" and I had to go over it several times. Then we did a poem that took another 5 minutes.

After this I asked who in the room could do addition and subtraction. Ida, Henrietta, and Charles raised their hands. And Timothy could add single numbers but his counting was filled with mistakes. I know because he counted to 83 before I could stop him.

I had Ida go over the ABCs with the Pospisil children, while Henrietta read to Timothy, using a Bible. Charles I found was very good with numbers, so I set him to drilling Andy, Jason, Huey, and Willa on simple addition, using a pointed stick and the dirt floor as chalk and board.

I took the rest and began reading a story from a history book to them, stopping here and there to ask them questions. Most did very well, but Mary, who was really too young to be there, always answered "George Washington" when asked a question.

Must go.

LATER

Just asked Henrietta to recite 2 German poems she knows so the children can have a break and I can write some more.

As I said, everything went well for the opening 10 or 15 minutes. Each group was bent to a task quietly in their section of the room. Father often broke his classes up like this, letting those children who knew a subject tutor those who didn't no matter what their ages. Every so often he would go from group to group to see if they needed help.

When I saw that my pupils had had enough history, I had the older ones write numbers on the dirt floor while Mary and Alfred drew pictures. While they did this, I checked the other's work. Everything was going just fine, but I felt surprisingly tired for having done so little. Then we went on to the next thing on my programme. Which was the singing of a hymn.

I chose "I sing th' almighty power of God" from *The Praise Book* because the words are simple and the tune is easy to remember. It was a struggle, since only a few students had ever heard it sung before. But after 15 minutes we were able to sing the opening 2 verses loud enough to shake the roof rafters. And they really did shake since Mr. Tyson wasn't much of a builder.

LATER STILL

My head is spinning and here is why. When Henrietta finished her poems, I checked Father's watch. We had used up only 55 minutes. Still over half an hour until recess! I plugged along and managed to keep everyone busy and working for another 15 minutes. But it wasn't enough.

Alfred started crying over some slight or other. Since none of the Pospisils spoke English, it was hard to figure out what had happened or how to stop the wailing Alfred, who had kicked at Nora and then me several times.

While this was happening in one corner, Jason and Huey began arguing loudly too. I think just to exercise their lungs. I picked up the crying-and-kicking Alfred and went to attend to the Bock boys when I noticed that Edwin was methodically un-raveling a string from the saloon keeper's Civil War flag.

I must admit I was so horrified at what he was doing to our precious flag that I shrieked at him to stop.

He said it was already in pieces, and kept tugging at the string.

"I swear, Edwin, if you don't —" That's when I noticed that Fred was gone, as was Carl. I asked where they were and Edwin jerked his thumb toward the door and with his usual sly smile said they went for a walk.

I started to call for Carl and Fred, but a kick to my chest from the struggling Alfred took the wind right out of me. "Alfred, stop! Nora, help me with Alfred!"

Charles screamed for everyone to shut up. He meant to be helpful but all he did was frighten the youngest children, not to mention me, and Alfred cried even louder.

And then the door filled up with a large shadow. Too big to be either Fred or Carl or any of my students.

"What is going on here, Miss Price? Is this what you consider an orderly class?"

"No, Mr. Gaddis," I said, handing Alfred to Nora. "We were . . . just getting ready for . . . recess." Why, I wondered, couldn't he have stopped by while we were all singing?

"And the 2 boys out here?" he asked.

Stay calm and think fast, Sarah Jane, I commanded myself. Before I could say a word, Ida told him that Carl had to use the outhouse, except that we didn't have one, she pointed out. She explained that Fred had to go along in case any Indians showed up. "Isn't that right, Miss Price?"

Said yes and asked Ida to be seated — and silently thanked her for saving me. When I turned back to Mr. Gaddis he didn't seem quite so full of anger, though he certainly wasn't happy when he said he wanted to speak to me outside. I was almost out the door with him when he asked, "Aren't you forgetting something?" He nodded in the direction of my students.

I stammered yes and asked Charles to please read aloud the first story in *McGuffey* when Ida blurted out that she thought she was the read-alouder.

"Ida," I said in a quiet but threatening tone.

"Sorry," Ida said. "Um, Miss Price."

Carl and Fred were hovering behind Mr. Gaddis, clearly

frightened that he'd caught them misbehaving. I ordered them to their seats before Mr. Gaddis could ask them any questions. All I needed was to have them say something that showed Mr. Gaddis I was lying.

When we were a little distance from my schoolhouse, Mr. Gaddis turned and faced me with a stern expression. He then told me that he wasn't surprised at all to find my class so out of control, and that I was clearly too young and inexperienced.

I was feeling very small and very angry by this time. I wanted to say, "You haven't even given me a chance, sneaking up on us," because I assumed that at the end of his talk he would tell me I was dismissed.

Then I noticed something. Mr. Gaddis wasn't screaming at me. He wasn't even speaking loudly. He was purposely talking in a subdued voice. Which meant, I hoped, that he didn't want my students to hear.

That thought made me blink and take a calming breath. Maybe he didn't mean to dismiss me after all. So I told myself, You are the teacher, to bolster my confidence.

"Mr. Gaddis, excuse me," I interrupted him. And believe me, that produced a mighty scowl on his face. "Mr. Gaddis, I agree that you caught us in a rough moment . . ."

"Rough," he sputtered, but his voice was still low. "I'd say it was a good sight more than rough . . ."

I held up my finger to interrupt him again. Told him we'd

done well all morning, and I'd explain exactly what we did in detail if he would like to hear. Added that he happened here just when we were about to take recess. So the students could stretch their legs and shout and run about some, which is especially important for the boys. I had gone on a while and I knew it, but I decided to press forward even though Mr. Gaddis kept opening and closing his mouth to say something. Like a fish gulping in air. "This is their first day of school. For some it's their first day ever. And they have to get used to . . . well, me and how it all works."

I stopped here because I knew I sounded as if I were lecturing him and he wouldn't stand for that very long. The funny thing is that when I stopped he didn't say anything immediately. He just frowned and seemed annoyed.

"Very well, Miss Price," he said at last. "I can let this pass. This time. But in the future . . ." And here he went on to issue a warning about stopping by to observe me on a regular basis and how I should have complete control, etc. I really don't remember all of the details, Little Book. I was too stunned at still having my position.

As he drove off, I stood at my schoolhouse door trying to calm down. The moment he was out of sight I went back inside and sat down. Exhausted, with a dull ache inside my head. Charles kept on reading and the children knew something was wrong so they stayed still. Even Edwin and Fred paid attention.

I glanced at the watch and nearly sighed out loud. Only

10:30! Still over an hour until lunch, and then there was a long afternoon ahead. How did Father do this day after day, year after year?

LATER IN THE NIGHT

Very tired. Nothing to say about the afternoon lessons other than we got through them without much fuss. I think Mr. Gaddis scared my students as much as me. Fred and Carl did wander off again, and Edwin pulled his box over against the wall and leaned back, not paying much attention. Alfred and Mary played very nicely together and I even managed to teach them a tiny poem which goes: "Old Dobbin's dead, that good old horse / We ne'er shall see him more / He always used to lag behind / But now he's gone before."

Another boarder came today, a Mr. Hibbert, and Miss Kizer seemed very nearly happy at dinner. She even asked me some questions about my day, as did the other paying boarders. Reverend Lauter sat still during this and did not talk until the conversation turned to another topic. I did not mention Mr. Gaddis's visit. Didn't want to relive it.

That is all for today. Which seems quite enough!

ℳ ℘

TUESDAY, FEBRUARY 28, 1882

Dear Little Book,

I left school with my students yesterday and today I saw my reward. Beer-box seats scattered about, writing sticks dropped everywhere and one — Fred Hewitt's would be my guess — stuck clean in the wall, the stove a heap of cold ash.

Lit the stove, then set to cleaning and sweeping and getting my little schoolroom back in order. I must not abandon it again. I finished cleaning up an hour later. Not just that it was a lot of work. It was sad to start the day with my room such a mess.

I made a resolution as I stood there. Before my students leave in the afternoon, I will give them clean-up assignments and in this way they will help me and also learn a valuable lesson.

Willa Miller did not attend today, and Carl was very late. When I asked why, he said he had chores to do first, but he did not look me in the eye and so I did not believe him. I could send a note home, but I worried about what Mr. Huftalen might do.

Because nothing went as smoothly or as quickly as I had planned yesterday, today I decided not to worry so much about my programme. Would try to follow it, but not be upset if we fell behind.

Which was a good decision. The Opening Exercise took even longer than yesterday, but that was because I wanted everyone to know "The Star-Spangled Banner" and poem by heart. Then I decided I would read a section from *Camp-Fires of the Revolution* by a Mr. Henry C. Watson. I chose that book because it has pictures and enough powder and bayonets to keep the boys content and quiet.

I was right too. Every student sat still and listened, and even the Pospisil children seemed eager, though I'm sure they didn't understand a word. I read this until I came to a particularly dramatic scene and then snapped the book closed. And did my students howl in protest.

"If everyone behaves this morning," I told them, "I'll read more just before lunch."

More protests followed, and Fred suggested that someone take the book from me and read on, but Charles said no one would touch it but me, and I said over the mumbling and complaining that everybody had to be quiet and that I would read more of it later if we got through our lessons. I also told Fred that I would appreciate it if he didn't call out in class anymore.

"Yes, Teach," he said in his usual sarcastic way.

For some reason that was even more annoying than anything else he had done so far. What would Father do? I wondered. Of course, I already knew the answer. He would stand over the offender and glare down at him — it was usually a him — and ask if he wanted to say the offending words again. Few did. No, the real question was what could I do?

"Fred, yesterday you and Carl left the school without

permission. I didn't do or say anything because it was our first day together. But this is our second day and I won't tolerate talking back or being disrespectful or any other nonsense." The look on his face said, "who cares" very clearly. I told him that when I read the book later he would chop wood outside and miss the story. And anybody else who didn't want to behave would miss the story too.

"You can't make me," Fred said. So far, every time Fred said or did anything, he did it with a little smile. But this time his face was defiant.

Charles said he would make Fred chop the wood and he started toward him. This was not going well, and it would be just my luck to have Mr. Gaddis show up again while the boys went at each other. So I told Charles to sit down in a loud, firm voice and said there would never, *ever* be any fighting during school.

Charles lowered himself onto his beer box, looking angry. Fred sat, looking very self-satisfied. Which was when I reminded Fred of Mr. Gaddis's visit the day before and explained that I would tell Mr. Gaddis about any student who was a troublemaker. And that Mr. Gaddis would probably report this to the student's parents.

Fred stared hard and hateful at me. I felt like running out the door and hiding. But I stood my ground and asked him if he wanted me to go to Mr. Gaddis.

In a quiet sulk, he said no.

"And you'll chop the wood?"

There was a pause and the silence seemed to expand and crowd that tiny room until he mumbled yes.

Fred did not look any happier than before or any more contrite, but he'd said the right thing. That was when I told him I did not want him calling me "Teach" or "Ma'am" or any such thing when answering me. "My name is Miss Price."

Here I lifted my eyes from Fred and swept them over the entire class. "That applies to everybody, please. It's important we learn how to act properly as well as learn our lessons." And then I thought of something else.

Tomorrow I'd bring in a little list of rules we should follow.

Which is when something amazing and totally surprising happened. Without prompting, a good number of my students answered, "Yes, Miss Price." The only thing that marred a perfect moment was Mary singing out, "George Washington!"

LATER

Talk around the table tonight was lively. One of the railroad men told about Black Bart's latest stage robbery out in California. That started more talk about the shootings in Tombstone and how Jesse James is still roaming free in Missouri.

"Makes me shudder to think those killers are all out there," Miss Kizer said, though she was still smiling.

The newest boarder, Mr. Hibbert, said he'd traveled all over the territories and hadn't been robbed once. He then asked Reverend Lauter if he'd ever run into any desperados.

"I've met many rough characters between the towns I visit," the Reverend said, nodding. "Some even in the towns themselves. The Bible —" how did I know he would get to the Bible one way or another? "— says 'they are around us and among us.'" He looked from Mr. Hibbert to Miss Kizer. "Sinners, that is. Some use guns to get what they want. Some use deception and a smile."

Felt my face flush and worried that the conversation would suddenly be about ungrateful children who defy adults. Then I noticed Miss Kizer. A few minutes ago she had been animated and lively, but now she seemed smaller and withdrawn. Her brown eyes had a distant look to them too.

Clearly, the Reverend's words had scared her. Maybe made her think about me and what might be out there, beyond the safe, wood walls of her house. It was the way he had looked at her, though — his eyes dark and intense — that made me ask myself if he said that to scare her on purpose?

The dinner talk moved on to other subjects. Including how my second day had gone. And Miss Kizer found her smile again. Though I couldn't help notice that it disappeared whenever she glanced in the Reverend's direction.

Helped Miss Kizer clean up. The railroad men and Mr.

Hibbert went out — they said to visit a friend, but I think they mean to visit the saloon. Reverend Lauter excused himself, saying he needed to read, and went up to his room.

Once the table was cleared, Miss Kizer told me I should do my list of rules. So I went to the parlor with a pencil and some paper. Grace pranced in, tail held high, and meowed loudly. As if to say "I'm watching you."

I sat there and recalled every time I had to stop teaching to say, "We don't do that in the schoolhouse." Then I wrote down the offense.

Could hear the clink of plates as Miss Kizer stacked them on the side table, the *tick-tick-tick* of the clock, the *whoosh* of the wind against the clapboards. The fire in the parlor stove gave off good heat and I began to feel drowsy. Must have been more tired from my day than I realized. My head nodded and my eyes grew heavy.

Miss Kizer came in and took up reading her Bible. She suggested that I might want to go to my room for a nap, but I said I was okay.

Thought my voice came out strong and wide-awake, but when I settled back into my rules, that drowsy feeling swept over me again. This time, I didn't bother to fight it. A tiny little nap wouldn't hurt, I told myself. I'll close my eyes until the clock strikes again.

Everything was soothing and black in my head. I had spent

most of my first 2 days as a teacher on my feet. It was a tiny room, but all the moving around in it, plus the trip to and from school, must have added up to miles of walking. It was more than just tired muscles I was battling. I was exhausted from worry — from being responsible for my students, from being new to it all, from worrying about Mr. Gaddis. Then Miss Kizer shifted slightly, sighed, and I heard her Bible snap closed.

My eyes flickered open, but I stayed still. Not moving, just watching. I wasn't being sneaky or underhanded — I really meant to close my eyes and drift into my nap again. But in the instant my eyes were open, I noticed that Miss Kizer was staring out the window. Out into the night and maybe beyond.

Was she worrying about all the sinners out there? Or the one in here with her?

Next thing, her face muscles seemed to tighten, her eyes darkened. Her expression began to change too — going from peaceful to thoughtful and then to sad all before the clock ticked 5 times. As if some awful scene had passed inside her head.

The sadness in her eyes deepened, seemed to be crushing out every drop of spirit in her. I was about to ask her if she was okay, when she opened her Bible again and looked at a page near the front. Very carefully, she touched it with her finger, letting it linger a few seconds.

The tension eased from her face and a faint smile appeared.

Flickered really. Fighting with but never quite conquering the sadness.

I had a sudden feeling that I shouldn't be there. That I was watching something private. So I closed my eyes and made believe I was asleep. But not seeing her didn't stop me from thinking about what had just happened.

"Sarah Jane," Miss Kizer said a while later. "Sarah Jane, would you like some tea? The dampness has gotten into my bones."

Fluttered my eyes open, then said yes, and Miss Kizer went to heat the water. Before she left the room, she placed her Bible on the table next to her chair.

I couldn't take my eyes off that book. At the very worst of her sadness, Miss Kizer had gone to her Bible — to a specific place in the front — and found something there. Some sort of strength. I wanted to know what words had produced the change.

From the kitchen Miss Kizer asked for my help with the cups. I headed out of the parlor to the kitchen, giving the Bible one final glance before I left.

WEDNESDAY, MARCH 1, 1882

Dear Little Book,

Got to school early today to finish up my list of rules. It was a struggle since I found myself thinking often about Miss Kizer, but finished just as my students began arriving.

Started the day by putting up the list of rules with 2 nails and reading them out loud. There were 11 in all, such as "No spitting inside the school" (which Edwin, Charles, and Nora seem to do a lot), "No talking unless asked to," "No leaving school without permission," "All hats must be removed" (Alrah's brown hat hasn't left his head yet that I recall), and so on. I have a clever bunch, so I had added a 12th rule: "Use your common sense and don't do anything you would not do at home or in prayer meeting."

Could tell that Fred wanted to say something smart then, but he held his tongue. It's colder today and I'm sure he doesn't want to spend time outside chopping wood.

Lessons went fine after this and everybody recited and answered questions at least once. Some whispering and idleness, but no one strolled away while I was busy helping other students. Which I count as a small victory. Read *Camp-Fires* for 30 minutes to close the day.

The children cleaned up the room at the end of the day and then left for their homes, whooping and running to escape. Ida and Timothy stayed to walk with me. Stood a second before leaving and scanned my room. Not much to look at, that's for sure, but it is working well enough so far and my scholars don't seem to mind. I took down the oil lamp, put it on my desk, and blew out the flame.

LATER

Supper was a strange affair. Oh, the 2 railroad men, and Mr. Hibbert talked away, but the Reverend seemed distracted and did not enter into the discussions as he did the day before. Miss Kizer was very quiet and I did not say a word — not wanting the Reverend to hurl another Bible quote at me.

At one point I saw Miss Kizer studying Mr. Hibbert with a frown on her face. He is a jolly sort of man, somewhat round in the middle, with wire-rimmed glasses, combed-down hair, and a ready smile. After supper and everybody had gone off, I asked Miss Kizer why she had looked so sour at him.

At first she said it was nothing. But then she said he's one of them. The men who are building the hotel. Seems Mrs. Tilling told her.

Took a moment for that to register because I was thinking that Mrs. Tilling is always the first person in town to know things. But when I realized what Miss Kizer had said and what he's doing to her, I asked, "Are you going to ask him to leave?"

"Of course not!" she blurted out, and she sounded really shocked. Then she spoke about Reverend Lauter's words, that there is no sin in casting out serpents, but she's not sure this is the same. Mr. Hibbert is a guest in her house and as much as it might . . . pain her, she'll treat him like any other guest.

Wanted to ask her if Reverend Lauter's quote yesterday —

about sinners being among us — had been aimed at Mr. Hibbert and not me, but did not want to remind her of the other sinner in her midst.

Instead I said that I'd tell that Mr. Hibbert if he wanted a nice room in Broken Bow he should try out his own tool shed.

Miss Kizer actually laughed at that, then told me to dry the dishes.

THURSDAY, MARCH 2, 1882

Dear Little Book,

I am so tired I will tell you about today very quickly and be done. 2 students absent, and Carl did not show up until near noon. Students worked fairly well, and played hard at recess and lunch. I could be mistaken, but I think Mr. Gaddis was about in the afternoon. Heard wagon wheels squeaking and thought I saw a shadow through the window. We were singing then, so I did not investigate and whoever it was disappeared.

Got home, had supper, and came in here to write and go to sleep. Reverend Lauter was tense and scowly all evening and apologized to other boarders for being distracted. Miss Kizer was chatty, but kept glancing nervously at the Reverend.

To bed.

☙ ❧

LATER

Climbed into bed, pulled the covers up nearly over my head, and felt quiet and peaceful. Not sure how much time went by, but it was later — maybe a lot later — when I heard a voice. No, not Father's. Miss Kizer's. Followed by the Reverend's.

At first I thought they were just talking. But before I could tell myself to go back to sleep, I heard the Reverend say, "The girl is one thing, Sister Kizer. She . . ." And I was out of bed like a flash of lightning and at the door listening hard. Assumed "the girl" was me because of the tight way he said it.

Miss Kizer was almost whispering, so the conversation faded in and out. But I picked up some of it. ". . . didn't want to leave Broken Bow and . . ." The words disappeared and I pressed my ear more firmly against the door.

"The girl defied you. In your own home." The Reverend's voice was lower too but that didn't stop him from making the words sound harsh. "She is young . . . but I will certainly have to withdraw my recommendation to Mr. Williams. But Hibbert. . . ."

"Reverend Lauter," Miss Kizer interrupted in a gently pleading voice. "Hermann, please."

I'd never before heard Reverend Lauter's first name. Hermann. I almost giggled. Knowing his name is Hermann Lauter makes him seem . . . I'm not sure what? More normal, like the rest of us.

". . . it would be rude to ask him to leave, Hermann. Terribly rude." She was still speaking quietly, but her tone was firm and strong.

Reverend Lauter said Mr. Hibbert was a coward who had come to do harm to her. For a second I thought I was back at the prayer meeting listening to the Reverend lecture about good and evil and such. Then very suddenly his voice dropped in intensity. "This is certainly your house . . . you set the rules. I will try to be civil, but . . ."

He left his sentence hanging there, that last word part exasperation, part warning.

They talked more, but not about "the girl" or "Mr. Hibbert." Civil is how I would describe their conversation, but not warm. Certainly not like it had been at the beginning of Reverend Lauter's visit. A yawn told me to get back into bed, but I decided to write this down so that tomorrow I will know it was not just the wind or a dream.

FRIDAY, MARCH 3, 1882

Dear Little Book,

Today all students were present and a very cold wind banged at the door and window. Students seemed more lively with their lessons and much more cheerful. After the Opening Exercise I had Ida read to the youngest children, while I drilled the others on spelling. Spent nearly 45 minutes on this, the time flew by so quickly.

Then students were divided into groups: some reading, some doing numbers, some geography. I used a map for the last group — Charles, Nora, Alrah, Edwin, and Henrietta — and had them memorize continents and oceans. Drew the map on the floor but without names and then tested my group. Even Nora and Alrah, who usually trip all over their English, could name them off as well as the others.

The only trouble came from the Hewitt boys. In the afternoon I set everybody to working quietly. I sat at my desk, thinking about Miss Kizer, when suddenly there came the sound of a cricket. At first, I did not notice, thinking a real insect had popped from the grass walls in the warm room. After another chirp or 2, a bit of laughter told me it was a game.

I suspected Fred and went over to him. But as I began to talk, another chirp from behind me sounded. Edwin this time. I approached him and there was still another chirp behind me.

I had a feeling this could go on all afternoon and already some students were not paying attention to their work.

Father would have caught on to the game from the start and put an end to it. But that wouldn't work for me. Not when Fred and Edwin were taller than me and would just laugh in my face. I could use Mr. Gaddis again, but decided not to. This time I had to figure out an honest answer. And fast!

"Class," I began, "it seems that summer insects have already arrived to sing to us. I think we need to catch them and send them outside very quickly, or we won't have any time to read *Camp-Fires* today."

There were puzzled looks from some, a few groans, and Willa Miller said it was Fred and Edwin. I ignored this and had everyone get up and search for our insect visitors.

Ida said, "This is silly because it's those Hewitt nits who made the noise."

But I just got her to her feet and sent her to look for insects with my other scholars.

The youngest children really took to the hunt and the older ones used it as a time to stretch their legs and chat. Saw Charles go over to Fred and say something to him, then Charles announced that Fred had found one!

Fred had his hands clasped together and a lopsided, sheepish grin on his face.

"Let's all catch a cricket — real or make-believe — and take it outside," I said, and that is what we did.

It took 10 minutes to parade outside, release our crickets, and then come back into the school. "Well, that was an adventure," I said, when everyone was back in their places. "I hope those critters are gone for good."

And they were. For Friday at any rate.

Later after dark

Snow is falling. It comes swirling down, doing crazy loops in the wind, then lands, and is pushed along. I watched it from the front porch and thought about Father. About the last time we saw snow together. In Iowa.

Father liked to take walks in the evening. Said it helped him digest supper and forget any problems he might have. We were out when the snow started and it came down heavy and made the houses, trees, and road disappear.

I was a little frightened, I remember, thinking we would get lost and never get home. We'd been in the town several months, but it was all still new to me. But Father seemed unconcerned and even quoted a bit of a snow poem. By Emerson.

My thoughts were interrupted when Miss Kizer came out on the porch. Said it wouldn't snow very long. Since it was cold she got me inside and then sat with her Bible. Before she commenced reading she congratulated me for being Broken Bow's teacher for one week. Commented how Mrs. Pelham said her Timothy and Ida came home every day and told all about what they learned and did. That deserved congratulations.

I knew how hard it must have been for her to say that, so it meant even more to me and made me blush. "Thank you, Miss Kizer. I know it makes things harder for you here. . . ."

"No, no, you shouldn't worry about that. You have a

school and your students to take care of." It was a very direct statement and if she had said it with a frown I would have taken it to mean "You've made a choice, so now you have to live with it." But she was looking at me differently. With fondness, I think. And I felt myself blushing again.

Wished we could continue talking — about anything — but Grace came by just then and distracted Miss Kizer and soon she went back to her Bible.

Sat a while thinking about my first week of teaching and what I might do better. Which is just about everything! Think I would earn a C for this week's effort. If that. Then I went back to thinking about Mr. Emerson's snow poem and the way Father had said the words that night in Iowa.

Pieces of the poem floated into my head, but I couldn't recall it clearly. So I got the book and searched until I came to "The Snow-Storm." In my head I recited the poem. "Announced by all the trumpets of the sky / Arrives the snow, and, driving o'er the fields / Seems nowhere to alight: the whited air / Hides hills and woods, the river, and the heaven / And veils the farm-house at the garden's end."

Father had said the words loudly that day in Iowa and even gestured broadly with his hands, as if he wanted to scare away the snow. I thought his performance was so silly, I started to laugh and the next thing I knew we were home.

"Thank you, Mr. Ralph Waldo Emerson," Father had said

to the sky before we went up on the little porch, "for seeing us home safely tonight."

It was nice to think about Father and not be upset that he hasn't appeared to me in days. To just relive a bit of our past together and feel good that it had happened. Am going to read the poem start to finish before I go to bed tonight. And remember that night again.

MONDAY, MARCH 6, 1882

Dear Little Book,

What a day, Little Book. Oh, what a day! There was an inch or so of new snow on top of a hard crust of old snow. I crunched all the way to school, stopping every so often to look at the way my footprints were following me.

The Pospisils did not come, I assume because of the snow and distance. Mary was absent too. Carl was very late and I had to mark him so in my book. Last week my average daily attendance was 12. But if the weather keeps them away like today I might not make enough to pay Miss Kizer.

The rest arrived very excited, with much sliding down the hills and snow and ice being thrown about. Took me a great while to get their attention and get them inside, and even then it was 10 minutes past 9 before the day officially began.

And what an antsy bunch they were. I tried to dangle

Camp-Fires as a reward for paying attention, but it seemed to have lost its power today. Still, we managed to get through various lessons and to lunch.

After eating, we all went outside to run around a bit and — I hoped — use up any excess energy. The boys had a notion that a beer box might make a good sled and I let them take one and try their skill. It slid along just fine, but whenever it hit a bump of ice, over it would topple and the student would go rolling.

This was all very good until Charles came down, hit a patch of ice, and went flying and rolling and tumbling — and crashed right into me! I stumbled backward and my feet flew out from under me and I landed with a painful thud with my dress up over my head. And, oh, how the children howled with glee at the sight of their teacher's underthings!

I can see now why they thought it funny, but this afternoon I was so embarrassed I got to my feet and yelled at Charles and the others and ended the lunch break early.

Students were quieter in the afternoon, but I did not feel much better, nor did I feel much like a teacher. Father never got bowled over like that! The only thing that would have made my day worse was if Mr. Gaddis had witnessed my fall. Thank Heaven, I thought, for small miracles.

❧ ❧

LATER

As usual, the railroad men disappeared after supper. A stage-coach had arrived in the afternoon, and now the Reverend and Mr. Hibbert were both reading the most recent newspapers from Grand Island without comment. All that broke the heavy silence between them was the rustle of the pages being turned.

Helped Miss Kizer clean up and she was surprisingly chatty with me. Asked about my day and my scholars. I may be mistaken but I think she has forgiven me for going against her plan and for not telling about the teaching.

We went into the parlor where I commenced reading and Miss Kizer sewing. Suddenly Mr. Hibbert cleared his throat and stood up. He wanted to make a confession, he announced.

Miss Kizer said she knew he was one of the owners of the new hotel. Not an ounce of nervousness to her voice. Or even anger. "Known it a while now."

Mr. Hibbert's mouth was open in surprise and he began to mumble something that sounded like an apology.

She waved his concern aside. "I admit I was troubled by the fact at first, but that has passed. We're competitors, Mr. Hibbert. Friendly competitors, I hope."

Mr. Hibbert apologized for not telling her sooner who he was. Miss Kizer accepted and said she might have done the same if she were in his shoes. Which wasn't true, of course. She would never do that. But it helped Mr. Hibbert to relax.

A smile creased his face as he went on about Miss Kizer's graciousness and generosity. "And may I say that as Broken Bow grows there will be more than enough business for us both."

"I pray you are right," Miss Kizer answered, returning his smile.

"Amen," said Reverend Lauter, though his eyes were flashing in Mr. Hibbert's direction.

A little while later I saw Reverend Lauter wince and look troubled when Mr. Hibbert made a joke and Miss Kizer laughed loudly. Is he jealous over the attention Mr. Hibbert is paying Miss Kizer?

When I caught Miss Kizer alone, I asked her if it was true that she's not worried about Mr. Hibbert's hotel.

"I'm worried all right." She laughed then and glanced out the window. She said in case I hadn't noticed, she worries over everything. Always has. But she tries to put some of the worries away.

I pointed out — gently — that his hotel might put her out of business.

She said maybe that would happen. But she couldn't stop him from building the hotel and she knew that to continue being angry would be un-Christian.

I said I'd stay angry and think up all sorts of ways to get even. She went on saying as I get older I'll learn to let go of as many of the things that trouble me as I can. Besides, being a good Christian has rewards beyond the heavenly. She looked around quickly, leaned closer to me, and whispered, "I figure that if I treat Mr. Hibbert kindly, he will remember it, and then, when his hotel is filled up and can hold no more, he will send some patrons my way."

That was smart, of course. But I think I would stay angry just a little longer.

WEDNESDAY, MARCH 8, 1882

Dear Little Book,

Carl and Fred did not come, and Willa said she saw them both up the path some. Went out myself and called until Fred appeared. Carl never showed up and I am thinking of visiting his parents to tell them.

Other than that, the day went smoothly — with reading and numbers and history and even a discussion of what China and the Chinese are like. The students were very excited when I told them that many of the men who would be putting down the railroad track would be Chinese.

Gave myself a B+ for the day. It flew by so smoothly.

The Reverend was out visiting all day and did not return for supper. Which made the meal more pleasant, not having his dark eyes to scold us.

One of the railroad men said Reverend Lauter had gotten very upset when he heard that railroad tracks would eventually follow his circuit. "He didn't like it that he wouldn't need his horse to get around," the man said.

There followed a discussion about how the railroad would change things — make places like Broken Bow grow, do away with a lot of the horse and wagon travel between towns. Mr. Hibbert pointed out that churches would go up in every town too and with them preachers would move in and the Reverend might not like that either.

Miss Kizer had been quiet through this, but then she said that he believed in the old ways, was all. But so did most of us out here. We came to escape what happens back in the big towns. The changes and such.

"And now," Mr. Hibbert added, "the changes have found him."

They've found all of us, Miss Kizer said, looking around at the men. She was quick to point out that most people see the railroad as a blessing. It would get the corn and wheat to market fast and easy, for instance. It's the things that the railroad brings that cause concern.

Mr. Hibbert pointed out that the Reverend could get a church of his own, if not in Broken Bow then somewhere else.

Miss Kizer said the Reverend told her once that he loved the rides between towns the most. "Out in the open, just him and God and his thoughts. He said it was his idea of heaven."

Can't say that being alone on the open grassland would be my idea of heaven. If anywhere it might be that other place. Still, it was sad to think that the railroad might take it away from him.

FRIDAY, MARCH 10, 1882

Dear Little Book,

The end of my 2nd week! Think I would give myself a C+ so far. Mostly because of Carl. He was late yesterday and absent today. Have tried to reason with him but he just says, "Don't need no books or learnin'. Goin' ta be a farmer."

I told him even farmers have to know how to read to find out how much crops are selling for and that he'd need to add and subtract to buy and sell things.

He just looked away and I had to go on with the rest of the programme. I tried to tell myself that maybe Carl was right. That he wouldn't need a lot of learning to use a plow and that if he showed up at school sometimes he'd learn enough arithmetic and reading to get by.

But then I remembered his parents. How they had doubts about me, and asked me lots of questions, but decided in the end to trust that I could teach Carl. I didn't want to let them down. Or Carl either. So now I will have to tell the Huftalens about Carl.

LATER

Reverend Lauter took his supper with the Gilmers tonight. He has been away just about every day this week — I think to avoid Mr. Hibbert and me. Miss Kizer does not seem to mind, probably because there are others here to keep her mind and hands busy.

SATURDAY, MARCH 11, 1882

Dear Little Book,

Bright sun is flooding the town and grasslands and melting away the snow. Miss Kizer said she felt spring in the air and even sang a song while preparing breakfast.

Met Ida on my way out of town to the Huftalens' and told her where I was headed and why. She offered to take me there on Henry, but I said no even though I knew it would be a slushy, slippery journey. And, oh, did she fuss and fume about Mr. Gaddis and his nasty rules. But eventually, she relented and I was able to be on my way.

The journey took a while and when I got there, both Mr.

Huftalen and Carl were out, so I had to speak with Mrs. Huftalen. Which was not easy. I was feeling uncomfortable about my mission to begin with. Carl might get a beating because of me and I didn't want that. But I did want him in school and learning and I didn't see any other way.

So I began. "Carl wasn't at school yesterday, Mrs. Huftalen, and I wondered if he is all right."

"Carl?" she asked, looking confused, "All right? Jah, Jah." And she shook her head yes vigorously.

That was how our conversation started and it didn't get any better as I tried to find out why Carl hadn't been in school. Back and forth with me trying everything I could think of to make myself understood. I even tried acting out a scene where I was Carl milking a cow! Didn't work — except that Mrs. Huftalen tried to pour me a glass of milk.

In the middle of this, I started to feel as if I was betraying Carl, who was just a kid really. Like me. Shouldn't I be protecting him from whatever his parents might do to him?

But every time a question like this entered my head, a voice said, "You are his teacher and you should be concerned." So I pressed on with Mrs. Huftalen until, some 5 minutes later, her eyes suddenly flashed concern and she said very carefully, "Carl not to school?"

I nodded.

She stood up then, and went to a window to stare out

across the melting snow without saying a word. Though she kept clenching and unclenching her hands. She was hurt, I could tell, and angry.

At first I worried she was angry with me, but then she smiled politely, and began making tea for us both. While we drank it, we made small talk. Or we tried to. After a while, I said I had to go, which was true enough. It was nearly noon and Miss Kizer had asked me to gather some Nebraska coal. So I said good-bye to Mrs. Huftalen and — in my head — wished Carl good luck. I will say a prayer for him tonight.

LATER

Stopped by Ida's and she seemed fine about today. Especially when I said I would tell her what had happened at the Huftalens'. But I made her promise not to tell any of the other students.

"Sarah Jane, do you always have to be the teacher?" she asked and then immediately added, "I already know the answer so you don't have to answer that." She held up her right hand as if she were taking an oath and solemnly promised not to say a word to anybody. Then she told me to start talking and not to skip a thing.

SUNDAY, MARCH 12, 1882

Dear Little Book,

Reverend Lauter is leaving. Tomorrow. He told us at the prayer meeting that he would be heading to Berwyn first, then to Ansley. After the meeting, coffee and cakes were brought in to give the Reverend a going-away party. People came up to thank him for his visit and to wish him good luck during his journey. "I will be back," he said in his big voice. "A few months maybe. I have too many good friends here to stay away for long."

He sounded so warm and cheerful and inviting. I almost went up to him to say good-bye like everybody else. But I also knew what it was like to have him pull that warmth away. Miss Kizer had been angry too but it had faded over time and everything seemed normal between us. The Reverend's anger never seemed to lessen. And I wasn't sure it ever would.

Slipped outside with Ida and we walked through town. Ida was chattering on about the party and I was thinking about the differences between the Reverend and Miss Kizer. We were near the river when we heard a voice and then Johnnie Hatter came into view.

We both froze and Ida gestured that we shouldn't move. Not that my legs would work anyway.

Johnnie had a cooking pot in his hand and made his way

over some rocks to the water's edge, where he filled the pot. A small dog — can't recall seeing it before but maybe he was the furry creature I'd seen in his arms — had followed him until he came to a big rock where it waited, wagging its tail and yapping happily as Johnnie went about his chore.

Both his hair and beard were long and wild looking and his clothes hadn't been washed in a while. He was chatting to himself and to his dog as he went from rock to rock and never looked up. When he got to a fairly level section of shore he placed the pot on the ground where his dog lapped it up eagerly.

His dog seemed well fed and full of energy. Which surprised me. Johnnie barely seemed able to care for himself, let alone a pet. So I guess Johnnie hasn't forgotten everything about normal living and such. The moment the dog finished its drink, Johnnie retrieved the pot and then the dog leaped up into his arms. The 2 headed up the edge of the river.

I wondered where the dog had come from and whether it had a name. That was when Johnnie stopped and turned his head in our direction. We didn't move, we were so scared. He was looking right at us — right into my eyes. And I had a feeling he'd known all along that we'd been there. Please don't say anything to us, I thought. And he didn't. Stared in our direction a moment or 2, then he and his dog continued their journey, Johnnie talking away as always.

Both Ida and I let out our breath together. Then I remembered the way Johnnie's eyes had looked. Gentle and pleading. As if all he wanted was to be left alone in peace.

MONDAY, MARCH 13, 1882

Dear Little Book,

I give myself a D for my effort today. Not for the way lessons went or for class discipline. Both were fine and most students seemed eager to learn. But the day began poorly when Mr. Huftalen drove up in a wagon and Carl climbed down and came inside, his eyes never leaving the ground.

Mr. Huftalen nodded to me and announced in broken English that there would be no more trouble from Carl. Then he drove off. I did not want to think about what had happened to Carl, but told myself he will be better for it in the long run. It was just hard to see his long, sad face and be convinced of this.

And then there was afternoon recess. I was playing with Mary, Alfred, and Timothy, while the rest ran up and down the hills around my school, screaming noisily and having fun, when suddenly I heard a cry.

"Injuns! Injuns!" And Fred came dashing wildly down the hill.

At first I thought it was a part of their game, but his face looked scared and he repeated, "Miss Price, Miss Price, there's a bunch of Injuns coming and fast."

I looked toward the hill, but saw no one. I remembered what Mr. Gaddis had said about this still being untamed country and all and that Indians were still around. By this time the other children were running toward me, some very frightened, others screaming that a Mandan war party was approaching. The youngest were terribly scared, some were crying. Alfred grabbed my leg and hid behind me.

I commanded everyone to run inside. I didn't know what these Indians might want, but I thought it best to be inside with the door barred when we found out. When I had them all safe and the door closed, I must confess to thinking some very bad thoughts about my school's builder, Mr. Tyson. The door worked well enough, but it did not have any sort of lock on it!

What would Father do? I asked myself. Probably go out to greet them and have a nice chat. Which I wasn't about to do.

Ida and the other children, some barely able to form the words, wanted to know what was going to happen to us and Charles said he should have brought his rifle.

Jason suggested throwing rocks at them, but very few of my students were eager to go out and meet the Indians face-to-face. They'd heard stories about what could happen. Not that I wanted to go out either.

I frowned and looked around the room, which suddenly seemed very dark even with the oil lamp lit and sunlight filtering through the curtains. I thought to jam wood against the door, but realized that all the stout pieces were outside. My heart was pounding as I expected a warrior to slam through Mr. Tyson's poor excuse for a door.

Move, I told myself! Do something! Anything!

I'm not sure how I managed to think to haul my table over against the door, but I did. Then I shoved the chair against the table, and had the older students drag over beer boxes until we had a good pile in front of the door.

"Get back against that wall," I said, pointing to the place farthest from the door. "You older ones take up our writing sticks and stand in the front."

Then I leaned against the heap of furniture and boxes, braced my legs, closed my eyes, and waited. And waited.

Nothing happened. No wild bloodthirsty war cries, no banging at the door, no nothing.

What were they doing? My imagination overflowed with ideas. One having to do with fire. Another had several attackers edging up to the building, rifles, knives, and spears in hand. But before my mind could spin the thought into something truly horrible, I heard a sound.

Not close by either. And not sharp or alarming. More like a stick being dragged along the ground.

Which is what it was. A horse neighed softly and then there came the faint crunch of feet moving over the snow. Next a young voice said something, followed by several other voices talking.

I went timidly to the window and peeked. There, some 200 feet from me, was an Indian family, father, mother, and 2 small children trudging along. With them was a large tan horse and a dog, each piled with great bundles of the family's possessions. Miss Kizer once described some of the Indians in the area, but I couldn't tell if the family was Pawnee or Lakota. One thing was clear — they did not look very bloodthirsty at all.

The 2 children spotted me, and pointed, before their mother spoke sharply to them. It was a single family migrating south, probably looking for better hunting.

Inside the room, I heard a chuckle that was definitely Fred.

That instant my head rumbled and thundered as it dawned on me that he'd played a joke on us. I wanted to yell, I was so angry. And I might have too, except I was still shaking and worried that I would stammer and make everything even worse.

Instead, I waited until I was calmer and then turned and told my class that it was just a family traveling toward Callaway.

I had the older students remove the boxes and get my desk and chair back in place. It was only then that I told Fred he was to chop some wood.

Fred blurted out that I wasn't being fair. That they were Indians so he didn't really lie.

"You set up an alarm, Fred, without being sure there was reason to. You'll know better next time."

He opened his mouth to say more, but I said that was all the discussion there would be. I held the door open and a very sullen Fred marched out to do his punishment.

The rest of the afternoon lessons were conducted to the sound of the ax biting into wood. Still, I felt very odd. Fred had played an old trick on me and I hadn't even suspected a thing. What else am I going to learn the hard way?

LATER

Reverend Lauter left while I was at school. Still do not know what I think of him. His words certainly touched many people, including me. It was his talk at prayer meeting that led me to see Father and to being a teacher. And his words helped Miss Kizer when she was feeling most sad. Yet there was something stern and hard about the way he judged us that made me uneasy.

I asked Miss Kizer if she would miss Reverend Lauter and she immediately said yes. She stopped to think, and I wondered if she was about to confess her interest in him. Instead, she added, "His words always help me feel renewed. I find new things in the Holy Book I never noticed before."

I felt so let down by that answer that my head did not

bother to think and I just asked if she liked the Reverend in a romantic way.

"Oh," was her only reply and her face started to blush. She was clearly flustered because she began straightening up the parlor — picking up the newspapers and *Harpers' Weekly,* putting pillows back in place.

The Bible says, "Ask and ye shall receive," and I decided not to let her escape to her chores this time. "Well?"

She said no, she wasn't interested in him romantically. She might have answered differently a few years ago, she added. Then a cloud of trouble entered her eyes and I wondered if she was thinking of back then, of what might have been.

Anyway, she added with a sigh, since then, she'd come to realize how very different the Reverend and her are. He can be very rigid about some things. Unyielding. So she will miss him . . . but not in that way.

I felt sad for her. Because I realized that way out here it would be very hard for her to find anyone who would be perfect for her.

Wednesday, March 15, 1882

Dear Little Book,

It is noon and most of my students are outside playing. Cold today with a fine snow falling, so they are sliding on the ice, which is made slicker by the light snow. I did not allow any beer boxes to be used because I expect Mr. Gaddis to make an appearance any day now. A few have stayed inside to finish their lunches and read.

All 15 are here today and the morning went well. Ida was working with Alfred and Mary when she blurted out in a very excited way that Alfred and Mary wanted to tell me something.

I went over, and Ida prompted them.

The 2 looked shy and giggled and Alfred said no. Ida leaned close to them, began whispering something, and my youngest scholars began to speak, though so low I couldn't hear. "Louder," Ida urged them. And then Alfred and Mary began reciting, "A B C D E F G . . ." And did not stop until they got to Z. And to prove they really knew their alphabet, they said it again and then again.

Victory! I thought. My littlest had taken their first big step.

LATER AT NIGHT

Where to begin and what to say? Best say it all and be done.

We had a very good afternoon. What there was of it. The snow continued and my students were eager to be out in it. As Charles said, there hasn't been much of a winter and this might be the last for a while. But I got their minds back inside by reading from *Camp-Fires* and then had a spell-down among the older students.

It had gotten darker outside, but I was able to turn the lamp up higher to fight off the gloom. The wind also picked up, but out here the wind is always picking up, so who takes any notice? It wasn't until I sent Edwin out for some wood that I grew alarmed.

He opened the door and just stood there. "Miss Price," he said timidly, "you should see this."

What I saw was a massive black sky pushing down on us from the north and a heavy wet snow falling and falling. There wasn't much snow on the ground yet, maybe ankle deep, which isn't much really. But that sky. It was big and scary and almost over us already.

As calmly as I could I said we should close our books and get the school ready for dismissal.

There was a cheer from my students, excited that nature was going to give them some free time away from their letters and numbers. But I remained nervous, watching that storm approach.

Seats were dragged into place, Jason swept the floor of all writing, writing sticks were collected. All very quickly as I did not want to waste much time. Henrietta and Nora got their sister and brother bundled up, while the rest got themselves ready as well. I closed the vents on the stove to cut off air and kill the fire, then put the lamp on my desk and blew out the flame. It couldn't have been more than 5 or 6 minutes before we were ready to leave, but when I opened the door the world outside had changed.

The black sky was over us — all around us — and the

wind was blowing and howling and driving the snow at us so hard that it made seeing almost impossible. It was a wild, white creature just waiting for us to step into its mouth.

Some of the boys whooped with glee when they saw this, and Huey sprinted out into the storm, his arms held out wide so the wind caught them and tossed him around. Which he seemed to enjoy despite falling down hard.

Jason and Carl began to push past me, but I grabbed them by their collars and told them to stay inside. Then I shouted to Huey, but the roar of the storm drowned out my cries. I motioned Charles forward and told him to go get Huey and bring him back here.

He did this, though not before being blown around like a leaf and falling over several times. When they were inside, I pushed the door shut and wedged a piece of firewood against it to hold it closed.

I announced that we were going to stay inside for a while. At least until the wind let up some.

Some of the boys did not like this, but they only protested a little and then sat down again. Regular classes for the afternoon were out of the question — no one was in the mood for real work. So after relighting the lamp and opening the stove vents again, I got out a book and began to read.

It would have been fun to read Mr. Emerson's "Snow-Storm" with its "Announced by all the trumpets of the sky —

Arrives the snow." That was certainly true today. But we had something just as good to read — *A Narrative of the Captivity and Adventures of John Tanner.*

This was the true-life story of a 9-year-old boy who was captured by Indians in 1789 and lived as one for over 30 years. We settled into Tanner's story and time went by easily.

Everyone sat quietly and was very attentive while I read, with some of the little ones sitting on laps. I think it helped that the many savage incidents Tanner related were accompanied by the savage sounds coming from outside. And the fact that he finally decided he wanted to stay with his Ojibwa family and not go back to his white relatives made many of my students gasp.

We were a cozy group then. The lamp glowed a warm yellow and the stove burned warm. We even had a little food, since some children had not eaten all their lunch. I was happy to sit out the storm in my school, but the storm had other ideas.

The storm pounded away at my school. I had Henrietta read and I took a little rest. I stood away from the group and leaned against the wall, and felt it shaking and quivering.

That worried me. But not as much as when the wall behind my desk — the one held up by pieces of wood — began to pull away from the roof. Only a little at first, just a few inches, but enough to let a cold gust rush in and cause the lamp flame to flicker.

My students grew alarmed at this and so did I. I moved them all back away from the crack and moved the lamp too. This helped us, but then the wind seemed to increase its angry roar and began ripping and pulling and tearing at the roof, lifting it an inch or so, then dropping it. Lifting and dropping, lifting and dropping. The next moment, a piece of stovepipe detached from the roof and crashed down, clattering off the stove.

The stove and pipe were hot, of course, so I couldn't put it back together again. I wish I could tell that Mr. Tyson a thing or 2 about his building smarts. And Mr. Gaddis too.

Sparks were flying up and landing on the ceiling, and smoke that should have been going outside wasn't. It was clear to me that we would have to leave before the place caught fire or before we choked to death.

The children had sat listening with their cloaks and coats on, so it didn't take long at all to have everybody lined up and ready to leave. I put Charles, Edwin, and Fred in the lead because they were the biggest and could break a trail through any drifts of snow we might encounter.

Henrietta came next carrying Mary, then Nora following with Alfred. Ida was to watch over Timothy, though he protested that he didn't need watching over. After these came Willa, Andy, Jason, Huey, and Alrah, with Carl in the rear. Carl may not be very big, but he is certainly my most stubborn student and I wanted him in the back to help anybody who might lag.

Before we set off, I undid a length of the rope Mr. Tyson used to hold his rafters in place and roped my students together. As I did this I tried to reassure them by saying no one was going to be left behind. And I think this reassured them.

Then I tied myself on with a piece of rope long enough to let me roam up and down the line. To check on all my students. The only things I took from the school were you, Little Book, and the saloon keeper's flag, which I wrapped about Mary to keep her warm.

We were ready, and I kicked the log aside that was holding the door in place. That door shot open like a gun going off and a stinging gush of wind and frozen bits of snow slapped me in the face hard. From behind me, I heard the stove flare up as air hit it, but I didn't bother to look back. There was no point.

We stepped out into the storm and immediately my 3 leaders began to struggle. Not with the snow on the ground. It was only up to the tops of their boots then. It was the wind they had to push and trudge against.

When all of the class was outside, the wind took them and whipped them around. Even Carl, who had dug in fiercely, found himself floundering. But with some help — I ran up and down the line steadying children and pushing them forward — we began our march.

The first part was easy. Straight out the door and across the clearing until the ground began to rise sharply. Then turn right, though not completely, and go up and over the hill and continue in the straight line for about a half mile.

The ground is very uneven out near the school, so we spent most of this stretch below the crest of the hills. Which was good because it meant we didn't have to face the teeth of the icy wind. Whenever we went over a hill we got battered and thrown around and it wasn't long before some of the frailer students started to wear out.

"Keep going, keep going," I shouted to them. "It's not far to town now. Just a little more."

And they plodded on, my parade of scholars did, lurching forward on wobbly legs, sometimes stopping altogether because they couldn't beat the wind. It was hard too for me to tell who was who. The wet snow had covered them head to foot. But on we went, a white, staggering column.

When my 3 leaders veered to the right, I hurried forward to ask why. Charles pointed and said the town was this way.

I didn't think so. "We have to go farther along that way first, then head left."

Fred and Edwin agreed with Charles, and I almost went along with them. They had all lived out here longer than me and had roamed all around the landscape hunting and exploring. Who was I to disagree?

Then I remembered the scrub trees. They were right at the

turn in the path. So I decided we wouldn't turn until we found the trees.

We got the line turned around and moving again, though much slower. The stop had given some the inkling to rest and their legs weren't moving with much spirit. We were on high ground, really having a hard time, when I heard a call from the front.

Went up to my leaders and there, just barely visible in the swirling, wind-driven white, was a clump of 5 short trees.

I yelled to go ahead 50 feet and then turn.

No one answered, I think because they were too tired. They shook their heads and went on, turning at about where I wanted them to.

To this point the wind had been at our back one moment, in our faces the next, and sometimes even from the sides. But when we turned it slammed into us from the side and we caught it full. Like the canvas sails of a ship. So our march was suddenly a swerving parade that looked as if we'd all been helping Mr. Bock with his still.

We were moving forward, so I didn't care how odd the line of march looked. Suddenly the falling snow grew so thick I couldn't see but a few feet in front of me and in a panic I dashed to the front and began counting students. All 15 were still lashed together.

Then the middle of the line suddenly collapsed as a ferocious gust sent Ida, Timothy, Willa, and Jason tumbling over in a heap. By the time I got there, Jason was being pulled up by his brother and Ida was doing her best to get Timothy moving too. I yanked Willa to her feet, but she was sobbing that she couldn't go on, not one step more and couldn't we rest a while.

Said no, we couldn't stop or we would all freeze. And I pushed her along a little roughly so she knew I meant it. Then I hurried — as best as I could — to the front and as I did I remembered a hymn from *The Praise Book*.

"Let my soul march boldly on," I sang into my leaders' ears until they heard me and began singing too. "Press forward to the heavenly gate / There peace and joy eternal reign / And glittering robes for conquerors wait."

I had drifted down the line, all the while singing and trying to get my students to sing. "March on, soldiers, shake off thy fears / March on, soldiers, your reward is near / March on, March on, March on!"

It was hard to tell how many were singing, but I knew I felt a stirring inside. Part energy, part determination, part anger that the wind and snow were doing this to us. "March on, soldiers, shake off thy fears / March on, soldiers, your . . ." And then I went ankle deep into a stream of icy-cold water. Which might have annoyed me even more except that I knew this meant houses were near. The Womeldorfs' and Millers', and then the town.

Yelled to Charles that we only had to go a few hundred feet more and we're home. And that word — home — sounded so very comforting and inviting.

He nodded and turned, and I heard a very faint, "March on, soldiers, shake off your fears," drifting back to me.

The others, of course, had to follow, and we lurched ahead and toward town. The first place we came to belonged to the Womeldorfs. Mr. and Mrs. Womeldorf greeted us at the door and got Henrietta and Mary inside.

They wanted all of us to stay with them through the storm, but I wanted to get my students home and said we'd go on. My plan was to take the Pospisils to Miss Kizer's, but Mrs. Womeldorf wouldn't hear it and pulled them inside too.

On we went and I think being so near home gave everyone strength, even Willa. She was home next, and then Charles. Ida and Timothy came after this, followed by Jason and Huey. Mrs. Bock spotted Carl and took him in too. "If the storm doesn't take the roof off," she said, "those 3 boys will."

After this, I got Fred and Edwin home, and thanked them for helping to lead. Fred said it had been fun and that he hoped he could do it again soon.

Finally, it was my turn to get home. Up the path I went,

humming the marching song. We were lucky then, I thought, to have the roof come off so early in the storm. If it had taken longer and more snow had piled up, we'd still be out there trying to break a trail through it.

My foot hit something hard. I kicked at the snow and ice, then pulled out a piece of flat, rectangular board. When I turned it over I saw it read THE FUTURE SITE OF THE GRAND PARADISE HOTEL.

Tucked it under my arm and headed for Miss Kizer's. Minutes later, I came thumping up onto the porch and pounded on the door, which flew open a second later.

Mr. Hibbert pulled me inside and closed the door. Miss Kizer was right there too, asking why I didn't stay put until the morning.

Told them the roof went. One of the railroad men poured me a glass of something that stung my throat as soon as I took a sip. It was awful tasting, but I drank it down. Miss Kizer brushed off the snow, got my cloak off, and started rubbing my cheeks to put color in them.

"It must have been awful," she said, then in alarm she asked, "and the children . . . are they . . ."

Everybody was fine, I managed to say. Got each one home or to a warm house.

And then a great wave of tiredness fell on my shoulders and I yawned.

Miss Kizer commanded me to get right to bed while she got me something warm to eat. When I got up I handed Mr. Hibbert his sign.

He looked at it, smiled, and said he hoped those fellows can build a hotel that holds together.

Then I went into my room, warmed my numb fingers and wrote this all down. If I waited until after I sleep, a lot of the details will have gone away like so many snowflakes driven by the wind. But now that I'm done, I am going to sleep 100 hours in a row. Maybe even 1000!

FRIDAY, MARCH 17, 1882

Dear Little Book,

Did not sleep 100 hours, but did sleep away most of yesterday. When I woke up, which was in the afternoon, Miss Kizer gave me very hot soup to fight off a chill. Who am I to argue? I drank it and was soon asleep again.

Later, after I had gotten up and dressed, Dr. Merriwether, Mr. Pelham, and Mr. Tilling stopped by to thank me for what I'd done. I said it was nothing, but even Mr. Tilling said I shouldn't underestimate my bravery, that had been a killer storm.

Seems all of my students had told stories about the storm hitting, the school falling apart, and how I'd lined them up and marched them home. I had a feeling that some of those stories could have appeared in *McGuffey's Eclectic Reader,* they were so outlandish. Ida, it seems, has not stopped talking about our adventure since the night of the blizzard, which wasn't that unusual when you think of it.

Mr. Pelham told me that some school board members had gone to the school and found it was beyond repair. That the wall had completely collapsed and most of the roof was on the floor.

I expected that the building was a loss, but when Mr. Pelham made it real, I felt sad all over.

Dr. Merriwether rushed to tell me that they would find another school for me so classes would go on.

Mr. Tilling cleared his throat. "We think we can convince the others that you deserve to be paid while we search for a new school." He seemed a bit shy when he added, "it's the least we can do for your saving the children."

They had brought along all of our books, most of which were wet and stained. Miss Kizer took them and hurried to the kitchen to dry them off.

Then the men rose to leave. But before they were out the door, Mr. Pelham stopped and searched in his pockets. Said that when they'd inspected the school they had found something they knew I would want.

It was Father's pocket watch and it was still ticking along despite the cold and wet and snow. I thanked Mr. Pelham and after I was alone I sat for the longest time watching the second hand moving around the numbers.

That was when I realized that I hadn't thought of Father since before the storm began. Hadn't wondered what he would do during the storm or whether he would think I'd done right. I wasn't upset, though. Just a little surprised and maybe a little proud that I'd done it on my own.

I wound the watch, then put its glass face against my cheek. In a few seconds I could feel its ticking pulse as the seconds turned into minutes. It was a familiar and comforting sound. As if nothing in the world was the matter.

SUNDAY, MARCH 19, 1882

Dear Little Book,

Went to prayer meeting and stood right next to Ida. Even though Mr. Gaddis was there and not smiling. I was the teacher, after all, and I decided I could stand and talk with one of my students if I wanted to.

Mr. Womeldorf was the leader of the meeting this time. He began by telling us that nobody in Broken Bow had been killed and that he'd been in touch with relatives in Berwyn and that Reverend Lauter had arrived before the storm hit. Which was a relief to all. Next he read from the Bible, keeping the passages brief, and talked a little about each. He was not as dramatic or as inspiring as the Reverend, but nobody seemed to mind. He even offered up a prayer of thanks for the way Broken Bow's children and their teacher had survived the blizzard.

"Did you hear that?" Ida asked in a disgusted tone. "He should have mentioned your name, Sarah Jane. You should be famous for what you did. Somebody should write a song about you. And us too. I mean, we made it through the wind and snow too. But they shouldn't mention us as much as you."

I told Ida, it's over, so let's forget it, okay. It's going to be spring real soon.

Which was true. The moment the blizzard stopped, the sun popped out and the snow started melting.

"And there should be a book. That tells of our adventures. We'll call it *The Amazing but Absolutely True Story of* . . ."

Mr. Gaddis interrupted her when he said he wanted to talk with me.

The first thing he did was to thank me for saving all of the students. This time I didn't act shy. I said it was just part of my job. Like cleaning out the stove and helping students find the outhouse.

I think Mr. Gaddis knew I was poking fun at him, but he didn't do more than flinch a little. Next he told me the school board was going to rent the old Parker house and fix it up so I could have classes there. He added that Mr. Parker was a much better builder than Mr. Tyson.

He hardly finished that sentence before he said, "But I also wanted to tell you that we will start work on a new wooden schoolhouse just as soon as the railroad comes through. It might not be ready for the fall term, but it might be up by next spring."

Ida whooped so loud that people standing near turned to see what was going on. I just gulped and took a deep breath. You are the teacher, I told myself. You and your students deserve a nice school. And you deserve other things as well.

I asked if my new school would have real desks. He said yes. And a blackboard? Yes.

I could tell it was painful for Mr. Gaddis to say yes. Each yes meant he had to order something from Grand Island and that meant his school assessment would go up.

Ida joined in and asked if it would have chalk, erasers, pencils, paper, and books. "And an outhouse. Going out behind a hill to . . ."

Mr. Gaddis looked at Ida with a frown. "Yes," he said in a quiet growl. "It will have all of those things. We're planning some socials to raise any money we can't get from the assessments." He glanced at Ida, who, thankfully, did not say anything else. Then he looked back at me.

I hesitated a moment, but then thought, you may never have Mr. Gaddis and the school board in this position again,

Sarah Jane. As Father would say, you have to strike while the iron is hot.

"A bell," I said.

I could see in Mr. Gaddis's eyes that he thought this was the silliest thing ever, so I repeated my request again, adding that every good school had one.

"And I'll ring it every morning," Ida announced.

"A big bell, Mr. Gaddis, so everybody for miles around Broken Bow can hear that school is in session." I smiled and added, "Don't you think it's a good idea, Mr. Gaddis?"

I could have been wrong about this, and I would never say it out loud either, except to you, Little Book. But I could swear a flicker of a smile appeared on his lips. "Yes, Miss Price," Mr. Gaddis said at last. "A big bell is a very good idea."

LATER

He was near again. I know it. Father's voice came riding along, seeming to call to me. So I put on my cloak and went out the back door.

Stood in the back, my face to the wind, listening, hoping. I know it must seem strange that I still think I might hear him. But the Bible and Reverend Lauter both talk about the Devil and angels and Lazarus rising from the dead and such. So why isn't a voice possible? It could be real, if you believe in the others.

The wind whistled gently and the Womeldorfs' dog barked several times, then the night grew quiet. Yet something seemed to be drawing me out into the darkness behind Miss Kizer's, toward the river. But I only took a few steps. The sky was overcast, no stars overhead, no moonlight. Just a gigantic cold blackness.

But I wasn't afraid.

Minutes went by. I started to shiver and knew he wouldn't appear, wouldn't say anything to me tonight.

Since I was 9, Father and I had bounced around, from town to town. Mather, Pennsylvania; Tridelphia, West Virginia; Piney Fork, Ohio. Always staying for a school term or 2, then moving west for one reason or another. Through Ohio, Indiana, Illinois, and Iowa. Always west.

Father said he had good reasons to leave each place — the pay was too low, the students weren't interested in learning, the school board wouldn't repair the building. I always felt he just needed to move, to get away from his thoughts about the past and Mother. To find some kind of peace.

There was the creak of a door behind me and then Miss Kizer called to me, sounding frightened.

Told her I thought I heard Father. Out there.

Miss Kizer didn't move or say anything for a few moments and I expected her to tell me it was Johnnie Hatter again. Then she was at my side and telling me he was in God's care.

Said I knew. I did know it too. Finally.

She took my arm and gently turned me toward the house, saying we could both use a cup of warm tea.

I expected her to change the subject once she put the cup of tea in front of me. I looked down into the dark liquid, steam curling up gently from it.

"He's at peace in Heaven," Miss Kizer whispered, putting her arm around me and drawing me close. Said if Father could appear he'd want me to know that. And he'd want me to know he's proud of me.

And then a drop splashed into my tea and sent a tiny wave quivering against the side of the cup. And another drop and another, until I couldn't stop the tears.

"Let it out," she said softly. "You'll feel better for it."

Usually, I hate to cry. But this time I didn't.

Footsteps came from inside, and I heard Mr. Hibbert call Miss Kizer's name. She sighed gently, getting to her feet.

"I'll be fine," I told her. And you know what, Little Book? I knew I would be.

EPILOGUE

With a great deal of hard work, Sarah Jane's new wood school was completed in time for the 1883 spring term. True to his word, Mr. Gaddis made sure it had desks, a blackboard, books and supplies. Plus an impressive two-seater outhouse only one hundred feet from the building.

A bell was ordered from a Philadelphia foundry, a miniature version of the Liberty Bell. It arrived in 1884 and was installed in the bell tower just in time to ring in the 4th of July.

Sarah Jane taught school in Broken Bow for the next thirty-six years. When school was not in session, Sarah Jane went to Grand Island to take advanced courses. She earned her teaching certificate when she was nineteen, and her master's in education a few years later.

Sarah Jane was particularly attached to her first class of students and kept in touch with them for many years after they left her care.

Ed and Fred Hewitt each bought wagons and set off in different directions as traveling photographers, taking thousands of portraits of settlers in Nebraska, Kansas, Colorado, and

Wyoming. Ida's brother, Timothy, became a lawyer specializing in real estate, then ran and was elected to a variety of local and state political positions, becoming state senator in 1918.

Most of her students stayed closer to home, marrying, raising families, farming the land, or running local businesses. As he had predicted, Carl Huftalen became a farmer. Even so, he often thanked Sarah Jane and his parents for forcing him to attend school. Not only did his education help him negotiate fair prices for his crops, he discovered that reading was the perfect way to spend the long winter nights.

After some additional delays, the railroad tracks finally reached Broken Bow and regular service was established between it and Grand Island. Mr. Hewitt drew up a grid system of streets for Broken Bow, and wood and brick structures began to replace the sod houses and tents.

Reverend Lauter continued to visit Broken Bow for several years, though when attendance fell to just a handful he headed farther west. The last letter Miss Kizer received from him in 1893 was postmarked Alberta, Canada, where he was preaching the Lord's Word to workers for the Canadian Pacific Railroad.

Miss Kizer turned out to be a remarkably shrewd businesswoman. As soon as work began on the town's train station, she hired a crew and forty horses and had her boardinghouse hauled to a piece of land she owned nearby. One of the first things travelers saw when they left the station was a sign announcing THE KIZER HOTEL — CLEAN LINENS & REASONABLE RATES. Despite strong competition from the Grand Paradise Hotel, Miss Kizer did a thriving business and even had to enlarge her building to twenty rooms.

Sarah Jane and Ida remained fast friends for life. Ida completed elementary and high school in Broken Bow, after which she helped run her father's store — and received a weekly salary too. With the money she managed to save, Ida took a lead from Mr. Gaddis and bought the farm of a failed settler. She rented this parcel to a new settler and used the rent money to buy up other farms.

Over the years, Ida's land holdings grew to over 3,000 acres, almost all of it rented to farmers and producing crops and a steady income. Even though wood was now readily available, Ida chose to build her first house of sod. It was a massive two story tall structure, complete with two turrets and a wood shingle roof. Ida never married, but the rooms of her home were not empty for very long. When a young married couple was killed in a flash flood, Ida took in their orphaned daughter. Gradually, other homeless children would find their way to her until she was caring for eight hungry and very active children. She lived in her house until her death in 1941.

Sarah Jane never had much of a social life, preferring to read and write poetry when she wasn't helping Miss Kizer.

Then one day when she was twenty-five, she saw a lone horseman coming toward her school after class had been dismissed. It was Charles Denning and after he had dismounted and removed his hat, he said, "Miss Price, I believe I am well enough established in business and confident about my future to ask you to marry me."

Their wedding was attended by just about everyone in Broken Bow, with Miss Kizer and Mr. Pelham standing in as her parents. Even Johnnie Hatter and his old dog made an appearance.

Sarah Jane and Charles lived outside of town in a small brick house. In the morning he would head off to his fields and she would head off for her school. Every night they would talk about the day, discuss what was in the newspaper, and read. They had only one child, a girl they named Faith.

Sarah Jane grew comfortable with the prairie wind and all of the sounds it created and carried along. Her father never appeared to her again — not the way he did just after his death. But Sarah Jane often went out at night to feel the wind on her face and to listen very, very carefully.

LIFE IN AMERICA
IN 1881

HISTORICAL NOTE

Almost as soon as the first Europeans established colonies on the East Coast of North America, they began looking to the West for new lands to settle. At first westward movement was extremely slow. The dense forests were mysterious and filled with wild animals and rough terrain. Cold winters in the North made survival hard, while hot swampy lands in the South offered little promise.

Native American tribes claimed all of this territory as theirs, but they were usually willing to share it with the newcomers. At least at first. However, as more and more white settlers arrived to crowd them out of their homes, Native Americans began to resist the trespassers. Few people wanted to face a harsh land and its angry inhabitants, and so most stayed east of the great Mississippi River. In fact, some eighteenth-century maps labeled the middle of what is now the United States as the Great American Desert — a place devoid of life and value.

All of this would change in the nineteenth century. Cities and towns in the East grew, and demand for food and other items increased. This change was accelerated by an influx of European immigrants seeking freedom and economic gain. Exploration sponsored by the U.S. government, such as the 1804 Lewis and Clark expedition, brought back glowing reports of the rich soil and natural resources waiting beyond the Mississippi. Suddenly, the West — all the way to the Pacific Ocean — looked so inviting that editor and writer John L. O'Sullivan declared that it was "our manifest destiny to overspread the continent."

The urge to possess the western lands was so strong that nothing was allowed to stand in its way. When Native American tribes stood in the way, President Andrew Jackson signed the Indian Removal Act in 1830 to force them from their homelands. Even after this law was declared unconstitutional by the Supreme Court, the U.S. Army was used to expel the tribes. The Homestead Act was passed in 1862 to give 160 acres of government land free of charge to any adult willing to set settle on it; the transcontinental railroad was completed in 1869 to speed folks to these regions.

New towns blossomed wherever there was decent soil and water. Even a rumor that a railroad might build a branch line in a certain region could get hundreds of people to move there. After the best spots were taken, the less desirable locations were settled next. The vast, empty prairie grasslands were among the last to be claimed and settled.

Communities often sprang up many-days travel from a

large settlement. This isolation was why most people chose to travel with large groups. People from the same national background or with the same religion would set out for a particular spot together. One part of a river valley might be settled predominantly by Germans, while a mile or so away a Swedish, or Irish, or Norwegian town might take root. The sense of a community, of shared hardships and responsibilities, took hold.

These men, women, and children were tough and clever. When they came to the tall grass prairie lands, they soon learned how to live without wood. Large "bricks" of unplowed sod with grass on top were cut and piled up to form a house or barn. The roots continued to grow after the building was up and acted like a "mortar" to hold the pieces together.

Dried buffalo chips were an excellent source of fuel, and when these were in short supply, cattle chips, twists of dry grass, and corn husks worked reasonably well. Special plows were invented to cut through the thick, densely matted grass to expose the soil.

Even when a family had a roof over their heads, the hardships of the prairie often found them. The tiny, often windowless structures were stifling hot in the summer, while doors and gaps in the sod let in icy blasts of winter wind. Worse still were the unexpected visits from rattlesnakes and other creatures that found tiny openings in the walls. One humorous ditty tells what a night on the prairie was often like:

163

How happy I feel when I crawl into bed,
And a rattlesnake rattles a tune at my head.
And the gay little centipede void of all fear,
Crawls over my neck and down into my ear.
And the gay little bedbugs so cheerful and bright,
They keep me a-laughing two-thirds of the night.
And the gay little flea with sharp tacks on his toes,
Plays, "Why don't you catch me" all over my nose.

Two powerful forces sustained these people through these first, difficult years. One was religion, the other was education.

Religion helped even when people faced overwhelming troubles: droughts, grass fires, tornadoes, blizzards, grasshopper invasions, crop failures, and deadly epidemics. Whatever came their way was seen as a test that could be overcome by hard work, prayer, and an unshakable belief in the Almighty. Sometimes a group would have a spiritual leader with them when they established their community. Often, circuit preachers had to minister to several congregations, traveling from town to town until the permanent leaders arrived.

Education was another powerful ally to these pioneers. Many new arrivals were poorly educated and virtually penniless when they set up their farms. Knowing how to read, write, and do arithmetic was seen as a door to a more prosperous and easier future for their children. Recent immigrants especially wanted their children to attend school, not only to reap the rewards America offered, but to learn how to be good Americans.

All states, even the newest ones, organized public school systems, from kindergarten to graduate and professional schools. The goal was to produce well-trained and productive citizens. Because towns grew up in such isolated regions real teachers were usually in short supply. Eastern teaching colleges tried to fill this need by producing hundreds of certified teachers, but the supply never met the demand. Qualified teachers who did accept job offers often quit abruptly, citing the primitive conditions, lack of supplies, and very low salaries as reasons. Clashes with stingy school boards (which had to balance the demands of parents and teachers with very tiny budgets) often drove teachers to seek employment elsewhere.

Instead of abandoning the idea of universal education, these states adapted to the situation. They lowered the age and education requirements for teachers and urged communities to find anyone who might qualify. Local communities often interpreted these rules very loosely. A girl aged thirteen, fourteen, or fifteen years old might be asked to teach a handful of very young children. As long as she knew more than they did, it was hoped that the students would learn something valuable.

School might be held in someone's dining room with four or five students seated around a table with their teacher. An abandoned sod home could be turned into a school containing twenty, thirty or more youngsters, varying in age from five all the way up to eighteen or nineteen. Sarah Ballard reported proudly that her Rosendale, Wisconsin, school "had sixty-six scholars last winter from the ages of three to twenty-three."

A teacher would usually break these large classes into smaller groups, each working on a different skill. This meant that an eighteen-year-old boy who had never been to school before might be learning to read with much younger children. Older students often helped instruct younger ones, with the teacher moving from group to group to iron out problems or explain a text. A well thought out teaching program and firm discipline were all that kept such a diverse group of children from growing restless and rebellious.

Despite the adventures and obstacles, many frontier teachers cobbled together books, created curriculums, and taught year after year in the same communities. Their schools grew in size and quality, becoming real centers for learning. And what did they achieve? One teacher, Martha Bayne, surveyed her many years of teaching and was able to proclaim, "Victory came. The children that sat in those hard benches are now filling important positions."

The seemingly endless plains that lay west of the Mississippi River and east of the Rocky Mountains were known as the American prairie. In the 1880s, Americans left the East Coast cities in large numbers to escape overpopulation and the scarcity of basic necessities. When the U.S. government passed the Homestead Act in 1862, the offer of free government-owned land drew many pioneers out to the western frontier.

Because there were not many preachers living out west, they traveled extensively — rarely settling down in any one town or city — in order to serve the multitude of budding frontier settlements. They traveled along circuits and stopped in hotels or boarding houses for a few weeks before moving on to the next town.

Without much wood available on the American prairie, settlers used mud bricks lined with a layer of grass to build sod houses, called soddys. The roots of the grass grew between the bricks, creating a strong mortar to hold the homes together. Sometimes families built their homes into the side of a hill for extra support and for protection from strong winds. Women often had caged birds to keep them company while the men worked out in the fields.

Since wood was scarce, settlers on the prairie used the dried excrement of buffalo—known as buffalo chips or "Nebraska coal"—to fuel cooking fires.

Prairie schoolhouses were also constructed of mud bricks. Because the schoolhouses usually consisted of only one room, the classes included a wide range of ages. Older students often acted as tutors, assisting the teachers with the younger children.

In 1879, settlers started building on the land that lay along the Muddy Creek Valley in Nebraska, where two buffalo trails intersected. These trails were later followed by gold seekers, and the town that began to spring up there was called Broken Bow. As more settlers arrived, with the railroad hot on their heels, Broken Bow grew prosperous.

With the arrival of the railroad in Broken Bow, more people stopped in the town. Hotels, such as the Globe Hotel, were built to accommodate the increasing traffic.

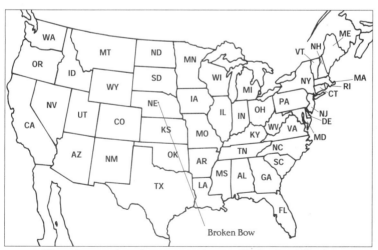

This modern map shows the approximate location of Broken Bow, Nebraska.

Prairie Cornbread

Ingredients:

    1 cup half-and-half

    2 large eggs, beaten

    1/4 cup honey

    1/4 cup corn oil

    1/4 cup packed dark or light brown sugar

    1 cup all-purpose flour

    1 cup yellow cornmeal

    1 tablespoon baking powder

    1/2 teaspoon salt

    1/2 cup shelled sunflower seeds, preferably unsalted

Directions

1. Preheat the oven to 375°F. Oil or butter a 9-inch-square baking pan. Whisk together the half-and-half, eggs, honey, oil, and brown sugar in a medium bowl.

2. Combine the flour, cornmeal, baking powder, salt, and sunflower seeds in a separate bowl.

3. Stir the dry ingredients into the egg mixture until you have a rough batter; be careful not to overmix.

4. Pour the batter into the baking pan.

5. Bake the cornbread for 20 to 25 minutes, or until a toothpick inserted into the center comes out clean. Remove from the oven and serve hot or at room temperature.

Serves 6

On the prairie, recipes combined simple ingredients to make hearty foods.

Salt Rising Bread

Scald 1/2 cupful of Sweet milk
to boiling heat. Stir in enough
cornmeal to make thin batter set
away until morning then take
1/2 pint of warm water & pinch
of salt, 1/2 teaspoonful of sugar
stir in cornmeal and thicken
with flour about like cake batter
set in warm place. Mr. Sawyer
adds a little ginger.

Recipe for typical bread as it appeared in an actual diary from the 1890s.

The Snow-Storm

Announced by all the trumpets of the sky

Arrives the snow, and, driving o'er the fields,

Seems nowhere to alight: the whited air

Hides hills and woods, the river and the heaven,

And veils the farm-house at the garden's end.

The steed and traveller stopped, the courier's feet

Delayed, all friends shut out, the housemates sit

Around the radiant fireplace, enclosed

In a tumultuous privacy of storm.

Come, see the north wind's masonry.

Out of an unseen quarry evermore

Furnished with tile, the fierce artificer

Curves his white bastions with projected roof

Round every windward stake, or tree, or door.

Ralph Waldo Emerson (1803–1882) was a preeminent poet, writer, and thinker in nineteenth-century America. He was and still is widely read and quoted.

Speeding, the myriad-handed, his wild work
So fanciful, so savage, naught cares he
For number or proportion. Mockingly
On coop or kennel he hangs Pariah wreaths;
A swan-like form invests the hidden thorn;
Fills up the farmer's lane from wall to wall,
Maugre the farmer's sighs, and at the gate
A tapering turret overtops the work.
And when his hours are numbered, and the world
Is all his own, retiring, as he were not,
Leaves, when the sun appears, astonished Art
To mimic in slow structures, stone by stone
Built in an age, the mad wind's night-work,
The frolic architecture of the snow.

ABOUT THE AUTHOR

Jim Murphy's inspiration for Sarah Jane's story came after seeing an old photograph of a determined-looking schoolteacher surrounded by her twenty-three students. Their beat-up looking sod schoolhouse stood behind them. He remembers thinking, "Wow, going to school must have been an adventure back then." From there he began his research in order to find out exactly what daily life was like in a prairie school.

Mr. Murphy is the author of over thirty books for children. *The Great Fire* was named a Newbery Honor Book, as well as the recipient of the NCTE Orbis Picture Book Award for Outstanding Nonfiction and a *Boston Globe-Horn Book* Honor Book Award. *Blizzard*, his follow up to *The Great Fire*, (among its many distinctions) was named a Sibert Award Honor Book, an ALA notable book, and a Jefferson Cup Award winner. For the Dear America series he has written *West to a Land of Plenty: The Diary of Teresa Angelino Viscardi*, and for the My Name is America series, *The Journal of James Edmond Pease: A Civil War Union Soldier*. He lives in Maplewood, New Jersey, with his family.

ACKNOWLEDGMENTS

Grateful acknowledgment is made for permission to reprint the following:

Cover Portrait: Gregory A. Coco.

Cover Background: By Winslow Homer, *The Noon Recess,* 1873, the Bridgeman Art Library International Ltd.

Page 167 (top): *The Prairie,* by Laura Gilpin, 1917, Amon Carter Museum, Fort Worth, Texas, Laura Gilpin Collection, P1979.119.8.
Page 167 (bottom): Man walking prairie, Nebraska State Historical Society, Solomon D. Butcher Collection, Negative #R63474-1892.
Page 168: Prairie preacher, Culver Pictures.
Page 169 (top): Sod house with cow on roof, Solomon D. Butcher Collection, Nebraska State Historical Society, Negative #B983-1784.
Page 169 (bottom): Sod house with birdcages, Nebraska State Historical Society, Solomon D. Butcher Collection, Negative #RG3698-1069.
Page 170: Woman collecting buffalo chips, Culver Pictures.
Page 171 (top): Sod schoolhouse, Nebraska State Historical Society, Solomon D. Butcher Collection Negative # RG62608-1774.
Page 171 (bottom): Schoolhouse oven, Culver Pictures.
Page 172 (top): Broken Bow, Nebraska, street, Nebraska State Historical Society, Solomon D. Butcher Collection, Library of Congress, Negative #RG2608-PH000000002457.

Page 172 (bottom): Broken Bow grocery and railroad supply store, Nebraska State Historical Society, Solomon D. Butcher Collection, Negative #RG2698-2662.

Page 173 (top): Globe Hotel, Nebraska State Historical Society, Solomon D. Butcher Collection, RG2608-2424.

Page 173 (bottom): Map by Heather Saunders.

OTHER BOOKS IN THE DEAR AMERICA SERIES

A Journey to the New World
The Diary of Remember Patience Whipple
by Kathryn Lasky

The Winter of Red Snow
The Revolutionary War Diary of Abigail Jane Stewart
by Kristiana Gregory

When Will This Cruel War Be Over?
The Civil War Diary of Emma Simpson
by Barry Denenberg

A Picture of Freedom
The Diary of Clotee, A Slave Girl
by Patricia McKissack

Across the Wide and Lonesome Prairie
The Oregon Trail Diary of Hattie Campbell
by Kristiana Gregory

So Far from Home
The Diary of Mary Driscoll, an Irish Mill Girl
by Barry Denenberg

I Thought My Soul Would Rise and Fly
The Diary of Patsy, a Freed Girl
by Joyce Hansen

West to a Land of Plenty
The Diary of Teresa Angelino Viscardi
by Jim Murphy

Dreams in the Golden Country
The Diary of Zipporah Feldman
by Kathryn Lasky

A Line in the Sand
The Alamo Diary of Lucinda Lawrence
by Sherry Garland

Standing in the Light
The Captive Diary of Catherine Carey Logan
by Mary Pope Osborne

Voyage on the Great Titanic
The Diary of Margaret Ann Brady
by Ellen Emerson White

My Heart Is on the Ground
The Diary of Nannie Little Rose, a Sioux Girl
by Ann Rinaldi

The Great Railroad Race
The Diary of Libby West
by Kristiana Gregory

The Girl Who Chased Away Sorrow
The Diary of Sarah Nita, a Navajo Girl
by Ann Turner

A Light in the Storm
The Civil War Diary of Amelia Martin
by Karen Hesse

A Coal Miner's Bride
The Diary of Anetka Kaminska
by Susan Campbell Bartoletti

Color Me Dark
The Diary of Nellie Lee Love
by Patricia McKissack

One Eye Laughing, the Other Weeping
The Diary of Julie Weiss
by Barry Denenberg

My Secret War
The World War II Diary of Madeline Beck
by Mary Pope Osborne

Valley of the Moon
The Diary of María Rosalia De Milagros
by Sherry Garland

Seeds of Hope
The Gold Rush Diary of Susanna Fairchild
by Kristiana Gregory

Christmas After All
The Great Depression Diary of Minnie Swift
by Kathryn Lasky

Early Sunday Morning
The Pearl Harbor Diary of Amber Billows
by Barry Denenberg

While the events described and some of the characters in this
book may be based on actual historical events and real people,
Sarah Jane Price is a fictional character, created by the author,
and her diary and its epilogue are works of fiction.

Library of Congress Cataloging-in-Publication Data

Murphy, Jim, 1947–
My face to the wind : the diary of Sarah Jane Price, a prairie teacher /
by Jim Murphy.
p.   cm. — (Dear America)
Summary: Following her father's death from a disease that swept through her
Nebraska town in 1881, teenaged Sarah Jane must find work to support
herself and records in her diary her experiences as a young school teacher.
ISBN 0-590-43810-7
[1. Teachers — Fiction. 2. Self-reliance — Fiction. 3. Orphans — Fiction.
4. City and town life — Nebraska — Fiction. 5. Diaries — Fiction.
6. Nebraska — History — 19th century — Fiction.] I. Title. II. Series.
PZ7.M9535 My 2001
[Fic] — dc21   2001020315
10 9 8 7 6 5 4 3 2 1   01 02 03 04 05

The display type was set in Edwardian Medium.
The text type was set in Caxton Light.
Book design by Elizabeth B. Parisi

Printed in the U.S.A. 23
First printing, October 2001
❦ ❦